IN ANOTHER LIFE

LAURA JARRATT

First published in Great Britain in 2015
by Electric Monkey, an imprint of Egmont UK Limited
The Yellow Building, 1 Nicholas Road, London W11 4AN

ISBN 978 1 4052 7119 6

57262/1

www.egmont.co.uk

A CIP catalogue record for this title is available from the British Library

Typeset by Avon DataSet Ltd, Bidford on Avon, Warwickshire
Printed and bound in Great Britain by CPI Group

Dedicated to the memory of my grandmother,

who told me stories on her knee

CHAPTER 1

Your text is where this story starts, Jenny.

I need you. Please come.

And so here I am: coming.

The plane touches down. I swallow and my ears pop. Dad and I unclip our seat belts and we shuffle down the aisle to the steps. When my feet touch the tarmac, I'm on English soil for the first time, just like you were six months ago. I remember you said to me once, as we travelled from Massachusetts to St Louis to visit Grandpa, that all airports look the same. I've seen enough of them now to say I guess that's true. But there's one thing that strikes me now, Jenny, as Dad and I walk through these night-time lobbies with all the stores shuttered down — and it's that all airports smell different. Especially when you land after midnight. I can scent the difference now. There's a smell of airplane fuel mixed with *here*.

So this is how England smells. We asked Mom so often what it was like. But she'd never tell us.

'Hannah?'

Dad's waiting for me with our cases on a cart. He's looking at me hard and I know I've been far away.

'Coming.' I breathe in again. England. It doesn't smell how I thought it would. Did you find that too?

There's a man coming towards us and he's exactly how I picture English people – he's wearing an expression as shuttered as the stores. Mom wears that self-same expression whenever we talk to her about home.

'Mr Tooley, the car is this way.'

He's a cop – a cop in a suit. Dad said they would send one to meet us when we got here. We get into the car and it takes us to a hotel. They'll brief us in the morning, the cop says. For now, we should rest.

I try. I get into a bed with stiff white sheets that don't smell of home. There's no Hobie to curl up at the bottom of the bed and wag his tail before he falls asleep. There's no kiss goodnight from Mom and Brandon. Dad's next door, as alone with his thoughts as I am.

And I know that the one thought circling round and round his brain is: *Jenny, where are you?*

I read that cellphone message from you again. It came the day after the cops told us you were missing.

I know you're out there, Jenny. What I don't know is where or why. You asked me to come so I'm here and I will find you.

CHAPTER 2

USA TWO DAYS EARLIER

'Mom, have you seen my running shoes?'

I came down the stairs in socks. In about two seconds I was going to be late. OK, it's hard to be late for a date with yourself, but running wasn't my favourite thing, especially on a wet day, and I needed all the motivation I could get. And that included sticking to my schedule. Any excuse could stop me from getting out there today and I didn't plan on lost shoes being the deal-breaker.

And that's the exact thing I was thinking about, Jenny, when we got the news.

Brandon was running up the hall from the yard, tossing a baseball in his glove.

'Not in the house.' Mom did that half-yell she only uses on

Brandon. She's never yelled at him properly since he got sick. She's worried about him, but we haven't told you about that. She's scared his remission is failing – he's got to go back into hospital for more tests. The crease between her eyebrows has got deeper and her clothes are hanging looser. She only picks at dinner when we sit down at the table to eat.

The house phone rang as she came towards me with the running shoes and an impatient expression. She answered it and our world exploded.

ENGLAND

I wake to a dark room with heavy drapes at the windows. It takes me a moment to figure out where I am.

The hotel room. You're still missing.

There it is: that sudden sick feeling in my stomach every time I think of you now. It's always there beneath everything.

I get up and shower mechanically. I'm going through the motions because what else can I do? Stand in a corner and scream? How would that help?

Get up, get dressed, be ready for the cops. That's my priority right now.

Dad and I chew our way through breakfast in silence. Toast and coffee – we can't manage more. The cops arrive and take us off to what they call an incident room. A guy comes in with close-cropped hair and a face that says he gets things done. Dad relaxes a little bit as soon as they shake hands.

'Mr Tooley, I'm DI Coombs. I'm leading the investigation into Jenny's disappearance.'

Dad nods and sits down.

'I don't know how much they told you on the phone so I'm going to run through events for you now.' He smiles at me. 'You must be Jenny's younger sister.'

'Yes. Hannah.' I shake hands with him too.

'We're glad you came. I've been told you two are close. We're hoping she may get in touch again if she knows you're here.' He turns back to Dad. 'Jenny's mother couldn't make it?'

'My wife had to stay behind. Our eight-year-old son is sick. He's been in remission from cancer, but for the last couple of months he's not been so well. The hospital are doing tests.'

'Sorry to hear that,' Coombs says swiftly. 'Did Jenny know?'

'Not all of it. We didn't want to worry her. She loves Brandon very much.'

Coombs nods. 'OK, here's where we are with the case.'

You've become a case, Jenny. I don't know how I bear hearing that, but somehow I don't speak, just clasp my hands together hard.

'At 8 p.m. on Wednesday evening, we got a call from the manager at Wolfscott Castle Hotel to say that Jenny hadn't been seen since the afternoon. We dispatched an officer to

Wolfscott. John Cadwallader, Jenny's employer, told him that this disappearance was totally out of character. Both he and Mrs Cadwallader said that in the time she's been working for them as an au pair, she's never caused them a moment's concern, so when she didn't return from her afternoon break, they were extremely alarmed. They and some staff went out to look for her. Mrs Cadwallader was worried that she'd fallen and hurt herself while out walking.'

Dad nods. 'She does like walking. Back home, Jenny is the kind of girl to pull on some boots and go off for a couple of hours in the mountains, but she goes with friends, not alone.' His hands are knotted in his lap as he tries to hold it together. I get that. Hearing these details of how you disappeared . . . left . . . were taken . . . is making me feel like throwing up. His voice comes out kind of uneven as he says, 'I don't see Jenny doing that without some company. Was she meeting someone you don't know about? When did you start looking for her?'

'With a girl of Jenny's age, we don't always start a search straight away as the suspected missing person will often turn up a few hours later of their own accord – a lost phone so they couldn't call or they just forgot to leave a message perhaps – but the Cadwalladers were adamant they wanted us to look for Jenny immediately. We talked to Wolfscott staff first to ascertain her movements. It was too dark to begin a ground search so we started that in the morning when she still hadn't turned up. In the intervening time, we put out a call to patrol officers in the area to look out for her.'

It makes sense, I know, but this makes Dad's jaw clench in anger. If they'd looked sooner, maybe you wouldn't be missing now.

'So what have you found out?' Dad asks.

Coombs sighs, an exasperated sound. 'Nothing, Mr Tooley. We've found absolutely nothing so far. Nobody saw her leave the grounds of the hotel. We've searched her room and nothing seems to be missing. There's no sign she was planning to go away and there've been no sightings.' He rubs his forehead. 'If it wasn't for that text message Hannah received, I'd be significantly concerned that we're dealing with more than a missing persons inquiry.' He turns to me. 'Do you have the phone with you?'

I hand it to him. They've already told me they'll need to examine it.

'Thanks,' he says, taking it from me. 'I want to run a few basic checks. It could be useful if Jenny contacts you again.'

'What I find hard to take is that there have been no sightings of her,' Dad says, swallowing his emotions as a cop comes and takes my phone away.

'That's not all bad. Often we get a lot of time-wasters calling up with false sightings. There is something I need to discuss with you though. We want to do a TV appeal. So far we've had officers asking locally door to door, but Jenny may have left the area and the best way to get information out to the public is via the news. I think we're at a point now where we need to do that and we'd like you to be involved. There's always a better response when the family speak in the appeal. But you should be aware that we will probably have a number of false sightings as a result and that can be hard to deal with.'

'But you do follow up all leads?' The question explodes out of me.

'Yes, we do. We always follow up.'

Dad sighs, long and painful. It's the same sound I'm making silently inside. 'So Jenny has disappeared,' he says, 'and nobody has any idea why, or where she's gone, and there are no leads.'

And that's the sum of it. As stark as that.

CHAPTER 3

USA, THE DAY WE HEARD
YOU WERE MISSING

When I saw Mom's face as she answered the phone, I thought they must be calling about Dad. Then she said, 'Oh my God . . . no . . . my baby . . .' And I thought it was the hospital about Brandon.

He stood there watching, bracing his little body for news . . . news that they couldn't treat him . . . news that the cancer was back . . .

'I need to call my husband,' Mom said in a voice that was nothing like her own. 'Can I get a number to call you back on?' She grabbed a pen and scribbled on the pad by the phone. 'Sorry, sorry, my head's not working. Is that the international code?'

It was only when she said that I knew it was about you.

Dad was home in fifteen minutes. He floored the gas to get back from work. We sat in the kitchen around the counter as he called England.

There was a lot of 'I see' and 'When?' and 'Why?' on the phone before he said, 'I'm coming over there.' There was a lot more talking, then Dad rang off.

'I need to call the airport,' he said.

'I'm coming too.' I stood up and set my hands on the counter.

Mom was so pale she could have been drained by a vampire. 'No, Hannah, you can't . . .'

'She's my sister and I'm going to find her,' I snapped.

Mom stared and stared at me, and I thought she was going to say something, but she didn't. Her face looked so . . . *wrong* . . . that Dad reached out for her, but she shook his hands off and ran upstairs.

I stepped in front of him as he went to go after her and eyeballed him. 'I'm coming, Dad.'

He locked his gaze with mine and we stared at each other in what you always call 'the battle of the same wills'.

'Fine,' he said in the end. 'You know her better than anyone. Maybe you should come. But right now I need to go check on your mom.'

I don't know what they talked about up there. I guess it's none of my business. All I know is Mom looked dead inside when she came downstairs again. It was that hard a decision for her not to come over there herself to find you, but she couldn't leave Brandon – we all knew that. We didn't talk any more about me going. Dad avoided mentioning it in front of her, but he told me when we were alone that Mom had agreed in the end.

So you see, Jenny, I was coming before you ever sent that text. You must have known that I would.

CHAPTER 4

Coombs tells us that what will help them now is to know more about you.

'If we understand what kind of girl she is, it may help us to find her.' He calls for coffee for us. 'The family is often the best chance we have of finding a missing person. They know things, little things, that we can't. Jenny may come forward herself after the TV appeal if you decide to go ahead with that. That's what we all hope. But if she doesn't, it could be the smallest thing that leads us to finding her.' He pauses. 'Often it *is* the smallest thing.'

Dad braces himself because talking about you is going to hurt. It makes it so much more real that you're not with us.

'Jenny is a good girl,' he says. 'She loves her family. She

was so great with Brandon after his chemo that I thought she might train to be a nurse. But she decided she wanted to work with kids.'

'My sister's always wanted to travel,' I tell him. 'She's always reading about different countries, especially England. Our mom's English so Jenny always felt like she had a connection here. She's a total Anglophile.'

Coombs nods. 'Is there family over here? Anyone she might have gone to see?'

'No,' Dad says. 'My wife's parents died when she was in her teens, in a boating accident. Serena's an only child and she made a clean break when she left England. That was nearly twenty years ago.'

I sniff. 'Mom hates England. She totally tried to put Jenny off coming.'

Coombs checks his watch. 'Let's take a break. I'll arrange lunch for you. You can take some time to think over what you want to do about the TV appeal too. Maybe talk it over together?'

But I can't help thinking that if only Mom had managed to put you off, Jenny, then we wouldn't be sitting here now.

CHAPTER 5

USA, TEN MONTHS EARLIER

Do you remember that Saturday morning? Mom was making brunch and you came into the kitchen waving a piece of paper.

'Mom, I found a job!'

Mom turned briefly, her eyes still on the eggs so they didn't catch. 'That's great, honey. Where?'

As you passed, I grabbed the letter from you.

'Hannah, no! I'm showing Mom,' you protested. But your protests are like being lashed in the face by a soft summer breeze so I ignored you and held the letter out of reach while I read it.

'England! You're going to England! No way!' I dropped the letter in shock and it fluttered down to your waiting hands.

Mom shoved the eggs off the heat and gave you her full

attention. 'What do you mean, England?'

You sat down next to me at the counter and took a waffle. 'I applied to an au-pair agency and they matched me with a family in England. These people own a country house hotel and they've got two young children. They want someone to play with the kids and watch them for a few hours every day so the mom can go back to working in the business. It sounds like a really cool job – look!' And you passed Mom the letter.

Mom wiped her mouth and took it from you. She read it with compressed lips.

'You never said a word about this,' I hissed and you flushed.

'I didn't think there was any point because I didn't think I'd get it,' you said quietly, your eyes resting nervously on Mom while she read.

But I know the real reason, Jenny: you didn't want to admit to me how much you wanted to get away from here and memories of Trey.

'Wolfscott,' Mom said in a flat voice.

'Yeah, I looked it up on the map. It's only fifty miles from where you grew up,' you said. 'I thought that'd be awesome – working near where you lived when you were a kid.'

'It's not near where I grew up. Fifty miles is a long way in England,' Mom said as she handed the letter back. 'I don't want you to go.'

Your lip trembled. 'Mom, this is a great chance. Please?'

'I don't want you to go.' Mom turned back to the eggs and began trying to save them from ruin.

'But Mom, why?'

'It's too far away. You're too young.'

'You didn't say that to Kacey's mom when she went to Australia for a year and that's even further.'

'What Kacey does isn't my business. What you do is.'

'It's a really good opportunity though. I get to travel and find out if this is what I want to do with my life. I thought you understood that's what this year is about for me.'

'Jenny, you have some crazy, romantic ideas about England. It's really not like you think. Yeah, bits of it are pretty, but a lot of it is a dump. Poky, miserable little box houses all crammed together on top of each other. The people never stop whining – it's a national pastime. They're cold and distant and most of the year the weather is wet and miserable too. You won't like it so put this silly idea out of your head. Call your brother, please.'

Mom served up the eggs and you got up to get Brandon. 'I'm going,' you said quickly. 'Whatever anyone says.'

I didn't think you meant it. I thought you'd give in. I guess I had you wrong there.

CHAPTER 6

'So,' Coombs says to Dad as we get back to the interview, 'Jenny's mother didn't want her to come over here. What did you think?'

Dad shrugs. 'I was fine with it. I thought Jenny should make up her own mind. There wasn't a big fight or anything. Once we talked about it, Serena came around.'

I think Mom dropped it rather than came around. She was never happy about the trip. Even when we said goodbye at the airport she was hoping you'd change your mind. You texted me later to ask if she was OK because you could see it in her eyes.

'What about friends?'

Dad smiles. 'Jenny's always been very popular, with lots of

friends. The house is always full of them. She's just a warm, loving kid and people are drawn to that.'

Coombs frowns, but I can't see why. That's how you are – everyone loves you. Everyone, period. You're the only girl I know who transcends high-school cliques.

'Does she have a boyfriend?'

'Not at the moment. At least she didn't back home. She was dating last year, but when Trey left to go to college they broke it off as he's three states away most of the year now. She hasn't been seeing anyone since.'

That's not exactly the way it happened, but that's the line you spun to Mom and Dad. They didn't see how your cheeks were streaked with tears night after night as you talked to me in your room. About how Trey didn't want to be stuck with you now he was in college. How you'd really thought he loved you. How wrong you'd been.

And I tried to tell you I could think of a dozen great guys who wanted to be with you. Probably more. But you didn't want to hear me, just went on talking about him until I wanted to plunge a knife into his guts for hurting you that way. Did you still miss him when you came here, Jenny? I don't like to think of you crying alone.

You could be miserable somewhere now, waiting for us to find you. You could be unable to come back to us. What if someone's got you and you can't get away?

Suddenly I need the bathroom – my lunch is rising in my throat. I dash out of the room.

After a while, a female cop comes to check on me. She gets me a glass of water and brings me back to where Dad's still talking to Coombs.

'They're very close, Jenny and Hannah. As close as two sisters can be. They're very different people and maybe that's why they get on so well. Hannah's the firecracker of the family and Jenny is our peacemaker.'

'Do you think if Jenny knows Hannah is here she'll make contact again if she can?'

Dad's chewing his lip. 'Yes, and we've talked about it. We decided it's important we do the TV appeal so she knows we're here. That's if she's somewhere she can even get to see the TV, because I don't understand why she hasn't contacted us again already. We've all tried calling her cellphone, over and over, but there's never any answer. We sent her texts . . . but nothing, other than that one message to Hannah. None of this makes sense other than she's in some bad trouble.' He turns and buries his face in his hands.

The text, Jenny – that's what we're all clinging to. Without it, Coombs might be looking for a body. One little text and so much hanging on it. One attempt to make contact and only one.

What if we're already too late?

CHAPTER 7

We're taking a break again and I wonder if this thing will ever be over. My head's starting to hurt. They've given me my phone back and I read your text again to make sure it's still there, to make sure it's real.

You're alive. You have to be. The words on my phone represent hope.

I'm thinking about the last time we were together. We were at the airport saying goodbye. You were crying, but you weren't sad. Yeah, you were going to miss us, but you were happy too. Excited to finally see England. You used to watch every English show that came on TV, read all those books by English writers. I was a little jealous you were getting to go and I wasn't.

Mom hugged you so hard I thought she'd never let you go.

I remember thinking how much you looked like her, that last time I saw you. Your long blonde hair was exactly the same shade as hers, your porcelain skin and big blue eyes inherited from her. Twins separated by time.

Mom told you a thousand times to be careful before you left through the boarding gate. You turned to wave, smiling through tears. Then you wiped the tears from your cheeks with the back of your hand. Brandon jumped up and down, waving both arms at you, and you blew kisses back. My eyes welled up. I never cry in front of people, but I could feel the salt sting and I turned away so no one saw.

I never said 'I love you' before you left.

I wish I had.

CHAPTER 8

The last set of questions, Coombs promises, but they're all for me and my head's throbbing.

'So you two were close. Did Jenny keep in touch while she was here?'

'Yeah, she texted me all the time and we Skyped.'

'Did she talk about what she was doing here?'

'Sure. She said lots about her new job, the kids, how awesome Wolfscott is.'

'Did she talk to you about any friends she'd made?'

'She mentioned a name or two occasionally. Cassie, I think, was one. She's one of the maids. Jenny talked more about the kids she was taking care of.'

'So you didn't get a sense that she was particularly close to anyone?'

'Not really. She was so into her job. I think she hung out with some of the college students when they were working at Wolfscott on weekends and holidays.'

'Didn't that seem unusual to you, given she's such a friendly girl at home?'

I shake my head. 'No, she may be really popular, but she likes to keep some stuff private too. She doesn't get close to people straight off, not about important things.'

Coombs nods. 'OK, so it was nothing unusual. Let's move on. What about boyfriends? Is she seeing anyone here?'

'No.' I glance at Dad. 'She was still kind of destroyed about Trey when she left. She wasn't over him.'

Dad snaps his head round to stare at me.

I shrug. 'She was more upset than she let you know. She didn't want to stress you guys out so she pretended she was OK.'

Coombs sits forwards, leaning his arms on the table. 'Do you have any reason to suspect Jenny may be depressed? Did you notice any difference in the way she was responding to you? Could being upset have spiralled into something more?'

I've been thinking about that, of course – I've been thinking about nothing else – but I still don't have an answer.

'This is important, Hannah. I want you to think very

carefully. Could Jenny be depressed and might that be why she's gone missing?'

They're both staring at me . . . staring . . . hoping I know . . .

I shrug and shake my head. 'I don't know,' I say finally.

Because, Jenny, I really don't.

CHAPTER 9

The car turns off a narrow road on to a track leading to Wolfscott Castle Hotel. A sign points the way. The family you've been working for have offered us rooms here for as long as we need. Coombs told us they'd said it was the least they could do in the circumstances.

Like you said, the castle takes my breath away when I see it for the first time. As the car turns the corner out of the woods, there's Wolfscott gleaming in the sun with its mullioned windows, turreted towers and warm golden stone walls. It's like nothing I've ever seen before. I gasp as I catch sight of the moat, a silver ribbon of water threaded around the castle in a protective embrace. The car sweeps over a drawbridge into a cobbled courtyard with a large central lawn, perfectly green like we always imagined England to be. We pull up in front of the biggest doors I've ever seen in my life. English oak, I guess – thick and heavy and studded with iron bolts. They're propped open and Wolfscott's given them a modern twist because just inside are automatic glass doors.

A porter comes to meet us as we get out of the car. He stops dead when he realises it's a police vehicle and then he sees me – recognition dawning on his face. I might have Dad's dark hair, but I look enough like you for it to be obvious who we are.

'Mr Tooley, Miss Tooley,' he says and that kind of freaks me out. *Miss Tooley?* Does he call you that, Jenny? 'Mr Cadwallader is expecting you. Please come through. I'll have your luggage taken to your rooms.' He beckons to a minion hovering inside the doors and the man scuttles out to get our cases from the trunk.

We follow the porter inside. It's so weird – a long corridor of stone walls and floor with those automatic glass doors at intervals. Crazy, like techno-medieval or something. I totally get how blown away you were by it all now I see it for myself.

The porter leads us to an arched wooden door that he unlocks. 'The family's private quarters,' he says as he ushers us through. We go down another long stone corridor with a thick carpet runner down the middle. He shows us into a large room with armchairs dotted haphazardly around well-worn couches. There's a small fire burning in a stone grate that seems to take up half the wall.

'Please take a seat. I'll send someone through with refreshments. Mr Cadwallader will be with you in a moment.'

Dad and I stare at each other as he leaves, both kind of stunned by our surroundings.

'Honey, I guess this is proper old England.'

'Yeah. Jenny told me how much she loves it here. Like she feels connected and totally out-there-amazed all at the same time.'

You were so completely buzzed by this place and you knew I would be too. That's how it is with us, both into stuff with history to it. But if you love it so much, Jenny, why did you leave?

A man hovers in the doorway, waiting for us to notice him. As we do, he walks forwards, holding out his hand to my dad. 'John Cadwallader. I would normally say welcome to England, but that's so terribly inappropriate at a time like this.'

Dad introduces himself too. 'David Tooley.'

I'm inclined to like your boss on sight, in that way you laugh at me for. He's tall with dark hair and eyes, tanned skin and a worried face, so I guess he reminds me a bit of Dad.

'I'm so terribly sorry. We'll do anything we can to help you to find Jenny. She's a lovely girl and she's taken fantastic care of the children. My wife's distraught about this. She's had the staff out looking every day, searching the estate. We feel so helpless.'

A maid, presumably from the hotel, comes in with a tray.

Tea and sandwiches, and I have to shake myself because it's all so different to home. That scares me. I can't help feeling that if you'd gone missing back home I'd be surer of finding you. It's like we've lost you in another world.

Dad and your boss exchange details about what the police have said and done, while I sit and eat some sandwiches and sip afternoon tea. They're very good sandwiches, but they should be ashes in my mouth. I feel so guilty for even noticing how good they taste. The tea's different to any I've had before – much stronger and actually a whole lot nicer. It came in a pot and Mr Cadwallader poured it out with a little metal sieve thing to catch the loose leaves.

The couch is squashy and I'm so tired from everything that I could fall asleep right here. I interrupt their talking. 'Can I get some air?'

'Of course,' your boss says and I scramble up.

I remember the way out, I tell him when he asks, and he says it'd probably be better if I stay in the courtyard so Dad can find me easily.

I bite back my words, that I'm not going to disappear like you, because I don't know who that would hurt more: me, Dad or him. All of us, I guess. So I hold my tongue and make my escape.

I go out into the 'courtyard'. The thing is the size of a soccer pitch and the castle is built around it. There's a central grass square with a huge spreading tree in the middle. I know this tree from your descriptions. I walk towards it because my fingers itch to touch the bark, to feel something you've touched.

You wrote me about this tree. You told me about it when we Skyped. It's really old, you said, and the bark is so beautiful. 'When I stand under the branches, Hannah, I feel part of something that has existed for hundreds of years.' And as I stand there myself, I feel that too. This tree is over five hundred years old, you said. It was here before they built the original house and probably here since the first ever building. That was a real castle, you told me. Yeah, I guess it would have been back then. You found out that it's an oak tree. And that's a symbol of England and you knew I'd understand why they picked this tree to represent the country when I saw one for myself. Right again, Jenny.

I run my fingers along the bark. Deep, old fissures. Reassuring. Just touching this tree makes me breathe slower. I stand with the trunk to my back, holding me up as I lean against centuries of sturdy safeness.

Over on the far side of the courtyard, a figure's going into a set of cages with mesh fronts. There are some weird little wooden posts on the grass in front of the cages and the whole lot is surrounded by a low fence. The figure comes out again with a bird on his arm. I squint so I can see clearer and confirm, yes, it's a him. Carrying some kind of big bird of prey.

He stoops and puts it on one of the posts.

A car swoops in over the drawbridge and pulls up outside the main door, just as we did not so long ago. A couple get out and the porter hurries to help them. Someone comes to drive their car away for them.

When I turn back to the enclosure, Bird Guy is putting another bird out. This time I see he's tying it on to the post. It flutters and flaps a bit, rising up as far as the strings will let it, and then it settles back on to its perch.

You told me about this too, that there are falconry displays at Wolfscott and that people hire the birds for weddings and parties. They even have owls trained to fly the wedding rings to the groom.

If you were here now, what would you be doing? Because I want to do what you'd do; that way I can *feel* you. Would you be with the Cadwallader kids in the fields behind the castle where you take them to run around and play on their little bikes? Would you be having a break? Would you be standing here watching Bird Guy, like me?

If you were here, right here, right now, I feel certain you'd be doing what I do now. Pushing away from this wonderful old oak tree, stepping across springy grass towards the birdcages, head tilted to one side on the approach, anticipating a welcome. You'd be smiling that smile that makes everyone love you and your welcome assured.

I follow in your footsteps, but I'm not you and I don't have your smile or ways. I find myself standing on the other side of the low palisade fence separating me from the birds. The falconer is in the process of securing a huge white owl to a perch. It takes me by surprise when he turns round – he's not much older than me, maybe seventeen.

He's more shocked than me though. He halts in his tracks and his mouth falls open.

'Who –?'

I know what he sees – you but with dark hair and eyes.

So Bird Guy knows you. How stupid of me. Of course he does. He works here so he must know you, even if just a little. This castle's not so big that he wouldn't have come across you.

His eyebrows snap down in a frown – thick, dark, straight eyebrows. Uncompromising, that's the word that springs into my head. He has buzz-cut hair and his skin is baked brown from the sun. His nails are chewed down, so maybe he's not as tough as his haircut suggests. Perhaps he's just the kind of guy who can't be bothered with his hair.

'I'm her sister.'

That's all that needs to be said. 'I'm sorry,' he says in a gruff voice as he looks at the ground. 'I hope she's OK.'

When people say that, Jenny, I realise again, all fresh and new, just how not OK you might be. I'm so afraid for you.

'Are you friends?'

He shakes his head. 'No. She liked to come and look at the birds sometimes. Used to ask about them. Mostly she'd talk to Steve, the guy who flies the birds in the displays. I didn't know her well.'

He uses the past tense and that tears a hole in me. He sees the change in my expression and turns away.

'I should get on,' he says and disappears back into the block of cages, leaving me standing there feeling stupid. I get the impression he's going to wait inside until I've gone.

What a weird boy. Did . . . do you know him, Jenny? Was that the truth he told me?

I walk back slowly to the hotel entrance. There's something about the last few minutes that's made me uncomfortable. I can't put my finger on it, but –

Dad comes out of the door and breaks my train of thought. 'Come on, honey. We're both feeling jet-lagged. We should probably try to nap. They've got rooms ready for us.'

I follow him in, but just as I go inside the door, I turn to look back. Bird Guy has come out of the cages and is staring after me – until he sees me looking and then he ducks back inside.

Then I know why I feel weirded out. It's like he knows something he's not telling.

CHAPTER 10

I lie down on a big four-poster of the kind I've only seen in movies. I don't think I'll sleep, but it's dark when I open my eyes again. Memory returns and there's that hole in my heart again, Jenny-shaped, like a cookie cutter punched right through me.

I reach for my phone to reread your text because it's the only thing I have to hang on to right now.

There's a new message. From you. My clumsy fingers fumble and drop the phone before I can finally read it.

Thank you xoxo

I'm faint, I'm giddy, I'm angry. I want to throw the phone across the room – how dare you just say that after all I've been through today? But I want to shout with joy too – you're alive, you're *alive* and you're probably close by.

I come to my senses and sit down on the bed. My first reaction was that you knew I was here – that's what your message meant. But maybe I'm wrong. Maybe you're just saying thanks for all the texts I sent you telling you I was on my way. And that means perhaps you're not nearby and you don't know I'm here at all.

My elation dries up like spilled water on a hot day – slowly, imperceptibly, but then utterly gone. I don't know what this means, but I do know we have to contact the cops so I go find Dad. I watch his face as he goes through everything I just felt.

Mr Cadwallader calls the police for us and they send someone round. Your boss insists we eat dinner before talking to the officer who arrives. I can hear by the muttered tones outside that the cop isn't pleased about that, but Mr Cadwallader is icily English to him about how exhausted we are and how we need to keep our strength up, so the guy reluctantly agrees to wait. And as soon as he does, your boss transforms into the gracious host again, offering him coffee and sandwiches.

I can't blame him – the food here is good. You told me that. I don't know how hungry I am until I start to eat and that sick jet-lag feeling resolves into 'not having eaten for a while'.

'Low blood sugar,' Dad mumbles through his mouthful. 'John's right – some food will fix us up.'

In the end, seeing the cop is totally uneventful. We meet him in the bar where he's reading a newspaper. Someone comes over to take our drinks order while I show the cop the message.

I glance at the waiter as he takes Dad's order. It's completely inappropriate, but I can't help noticing he is hot. He sees me looking and smiles before he whisks away in that unobtrusive, efficient way all the staff here seem to be trained in.

The cop is as bemused by your message as we are. 'Can I take this to the station with me to run some more checks?'

'What if she texts again though? I'll miss it.'

'We'll have to take that chance, I'm afraid. How about we let you know if any more messages are received?'

I agree reluctantly. 'Can I get it back in the morning?'

He nods. We're doing the appeal on TV tomorrow. I hope you see it — that's the whole point.

The sick feeling returns because I hope you *can* see it.

The hot bar guy comes back over to collect our glasses as we get up to leave. He touches my elbow as I pass — a finger-brush on my sleeve. 'I hope she turns up soon,' he says in a soft whisper. It's the kind of whisper that's not meant to be secret, it's just nobody else's business.

He must know you, Jenny. I see that in his eyes and I see that he realises I wouldn't want to talk about it in a public bar.

I whisper back a broken, 'Thank you,' and follow Dad out.

When we're back upstairs, after I've called Mom to say goodnight, I lie in the four-poster and think about everything.

Getting through tomorrow is going to be tough and I hope, hope, hope you call after you see us on TV. If you don't, I'm going to have to start doing some investigating myself. I can't just sit back here and do nothing – it's killing me. You know how useless I am at waiting. I'll start with some of the guys you hang out with. I need to find that waitress Cassie and talk to her. If we get back in time tomorrow, I'll do that – I'll start with her, I think as I slide into sleep.

Sleep is the only place where you're not missing.

CHAPTER 11

I hate everything about the press conference.

DI Coombs sits us down with coffee. 'Half an hour before we start. I'll begin by making an opening statement, then I'll hand over to each of you. Remember the impression we want to create is one that shows how worried you are that Jenny's missing, but that you're not angry, you just want her back.' He pauses and his expression changes. I don't understand why until he speaks. 'If someone is holding Jenny against her will, we want to appeal to their better nature so they'll consider letting her go. Show how loved and missed she is.'

Dad's ashen. I mean, we've all thought it, Jenny, but until this happened, I never understood the chasm between thinking something and hearing it voiced by a reasonable person. We die many little deaths in a lifetime with the things we worry about and never say aloud. When those worries are voiced, they have a power I'd never dreamed they could.

'I don't want you to mention the texts at all,' he continues. 'If someone has taken Jenny against her will, it's vital they don't know she's communicated with us. That doesn't just apply to the TV appeal – please don't discuss them with anyone. It's safer that way.'

'Is that what you think has happened – someone has her?' Dad has his fingers knotted in his hair.

The detective purses his lips. 'It's a real possibility. Those texts Jenny sent are very short and they don't reveal anything. That could suggest she has limited opportunities for communication.'

Coombs gives us another tip as my skin still crawls from what he's just said. 'Imagine Jenny . . . or whoever has Jenny . . . is standing just behind the cameras and talk directly to them.'

When it's time, he walks us into a room full of media people and sits us down behind a long table set up with microphones. There's a glass of water in front of me. The room falls silent as we sit down.

I look down at my hands in my lap – they're shaking.

Coombs begins. 'Four days ago, Jenny Tooley was reported missing from Wolfscott Castle Hotel. Jenny is an American citizen working over here as an au pair. She's eighteen years old and her employers describe her as utterly reliable and a lovely girl. Here's a picture of Jenny taken only a few months ago.'

He pauses as the screen behind us shows a giant you from the photo Dad gave the cops.

'Jenny went missing on Wednesday afternoon after a normal morning at work. She had a break of three hours after lunch and was expected to return to her duties at 4 p.m. She never reappeared. Jenny's employers say she hadn't been in any trouble at all and she'd seemed her usual happy self before she went on her break. Jenny's family say the last time they spoke to her she was bubbly and full of how much she was enjoying her job. Nobody knows of any reason why Jenny might have wanted to leave Wolfscott and not return. We are appealing to the public to report any sightings of Jenny to our incident room on this number.'

A phone number appears below your picture on the screen.

'We are now concerned for her safety. Jenny is five foot eight with long blonde hair and blue eyes. She's of slim build. When she was last seen, she was wearing jeans and a blue T-shirt with a butterfly on the front in rainbow colours. She was also wearing dark trainers and took a dark blue waterproof jacket with her when she went for an afternoon walk. Her hair was twisted up in a bun. She's believed to have headed in the direction of Wolfscott Hill. We would like anyone who saw her that afternoon to make contact with us so we can confirm her exact movements. It's very important that we know whether Jenny did take her usual route or not. I want to stress that this disappearance is very out of character for Jenny, which is why we are concerned for her safety. Please get in touch if you see her or think you've seen her. I'm now going to hand over to Jenny's father who has something he wants to say to his daughter in case she's listening.'

I can't describe to you my feelings. We watch these things so many times on TV. We watch the emotions on the faces of the families. We pass judgement on them too: that one's a good mother; this one maybe not so much. We think we know how they must feel: we don't. There is nothing that can prepare us for the soul-shredding awfulness of sitting there, sharing pain and grief we don't want to admit to because it kills the hope we're desperately trying to hang on to. We can either be brave and let all that show or we can let the numbness that brings a horrible relief wash over us and sit there, zombie-style, going through the motions and shutting out how we really feel.

Dad's brave. I knew he would be.

'Jenny, if you're listening, honey, I want you to know nobody's mad at you. If you chose to go off, we know you must've had a really good reason, even if we don't know what that is. We love you, baby, and we want you to come home. We all miss you. We just want you home. Whatever made you run away, if you did run away, it could never change how we feel about you. Get in touch, honey. Come back to us.'

He's crying, Jenny. Tears are rolling down his cheeks in front of everyone. Maybe you can see that. If you can, please listen.

His voice breaks. He has to do this next part, but it's harder and he's sobbing between every sentence.

'This is to anyone who might have taken Jenny against her will. You need to know that Jenny is a good girl who'd never hurt anybody. If you've got her, please let her go. Her family need her. She's got a mom back home looking after her little brother who's really sick right now.

'I don't know why you might have taken her, but please don't hurt her. Jenny doesn't deserve this. Maybe you've got no intention of harming her and, if that's so, please don't be mad because I said that – it's what any father would be scared of with his little girl missing.'

Dad's staring right behind the camera, as if the person who took you is there, just like Coombs told us to do.

'Maybe you've made a mistake and you're scared yourself to let her go. Please understand that all we want is Jenny back safe and well. Nothing else. Let her go somewhere where she'll be found. We're not interested in going after you – we only want Jenny home.'

Coombs told him to say this to make any potential kidnapper

feel a bond with him, like he and Dad could understand each other.

All too suddenly, even though we'd rehearsed and I should have known my cue, Dad's saying, 'Jenny, your sister wants to say something.'

I can see the cutaway screen at the side of the studio; the camera switches to me with the words 'Hannah Tooley, Jenny's sister' underneath. My breath catches, my lungs closing up like an asthmatic. My turn.

I'm not brave. You can read me though, even if the rest of the world thinks I'm a cold-hearted bitch. You'll know.

'Jenny, Dad's right.' I say it like an automaton. 'We all want you home. Please get in touch and let us know you're all right.'

If you can get in touch . . .

'I miss you so much,' I say in the flattest voice imaginable. Coombs stiffens besides me and I know I'm letting you down. I don't do crying in public, you know that. I don't do emotions in front of people, except anger. And now here I am, letting you down because once again I'm this stupid, shuttered-up thing. So unlike you.

I stop speaking. They're all staring at me. The pressure inside me builds and builds as their eyes fix on me, harder and harder.

I hate them. I hate their eyes. I hate that they're here when you're not. And most of all, I hate me because I can't do this one thing right for you.

'I miss her!' I shout at them, an explosion of anger, as I slam the desk with my hand. 'I miss my sister and I want her back. I'm so scared for her that I can't breathe sometimes!'

Coombs lays a cool hand over mine and my dad quickly takes my other hand.

There are tears on my face, Jenny. I can feel them and everyone can see them. Hot, savage tears.

I know what I'm supposed to say and how. Coombs squeezes my hand to remind me.

I look at that spot behind the camera. 'Jenny, we need you. Please come back. Please.'

And I can't say any more – there are too many tears and my mouth is salty with them. I hear Coombs whisper, 'Well done,' and I bury my face in my arms to hide from all those eyes.

You will know what this cost me.

CHAPTER 12

Dad wanted to wait around at the police station until the appeal went out on TV for the first time. They broadcast it on the national news at noon. I guess he hoped there'd be loads of response straight away. Me, I couldn't begin to imagine what might happen next. They fed us again. Cop food is pretty bad, but it didn't matter. Today everything tastes like the bottom of a hamster cage anyway.

There are some calls from the public. Nothing specific they can follow up, Coombs says – just people who'd seen you walking that way on other days, but it's now confirmed as a route you knew. It's a nice day though and Coombs thinks there won't be too many people stuck in front of the TV, watching news. He tells us we should go back to Wolfscott and get some fresh air ourselves. He'll call later if anything comes in and if there aren't any leads then he'll call anyway so at least we know that much.

So we head back to the hotel. The cops find us a car quickly and the driver has exactly the right expression of non-intrusive sympathy.

The sun's warm today, Jenny. I hope you can see that wherever you are. I keep thinking right now of all those stories you see on CNN about crazies who've locked girls up in their basements for decades. It scares the hell out of me to think, even in my wildest moments, that could be happening to you.

I wash my face to get rid of the tear stains, but I feel dirty all over as I remember how I lost it in front of all those people so I get in the shower and scrub clean. I put some shorts and a T-shirt on and head downstairs. That file they leave in the hotel room tells me there's a garden out back that catches the afternoon and evening sun so I go in search of it.

It turns out to be a large lawn the size of a field, dotted with dwarf trees. There's sunloungers up on a terrace, but the last thing I want is to be near other people. I walk down the grassy slope that eventually leads to a little lake. When I skirt to the left, it brings me to a quiet area where I can see the water, but I'm sheltered from the people back on the terrace. No one to watch me; no one to talk in low voices about what might have happened to you. I can't bear to hear that right now.

I lie on soft grass and close my eyes. It's incredible that only last week I was sitting in our old tree house in our yard back home, thinking about what in hell I was going to do with my life and envying you because you seemed to have that all figured out. I can't remember exactly when it was . . . yeah, it must have been the day before the bomb dropped. It feels like a lifetime ago now. I was thinking about you, wondering what you'd be doing, and in the space between those thoughts I breathed in long, slow breaths of home. The tree house still smelled the same – that spicy, resinous scent that used to cling to our clothes when we were kids and follow us to bed at night until we put our PJs on. It was the first time I'd been up there since you left. Brandon doesn't feel the same about it as we did. To him, it's a wooden box up a tree with no space to throw a ball around. For us, it was where we traded our secrets. I could still hear those secrets as I sat there. They were hiding in the wood whispering to me.

And I remember. We were in the tree house together. You were thirteen and I was eleven, all knobby knees and straggly hair. You got your curves early, along with perfect skin and suddenly co-operative hair and colt-long legs. You were beautiful, I realised as we sat there together, and I felt far from you in a way I never had before.

'I think I really like Drew,' you said and I struggled to

remember who Drew might be. You blushed. 'And I think he really likes me too. Kayla says he does. He told her he thought I was pretty.'

You were more than pretty; you were radiant. I desperately hoped that this boy whose face I couldn't even recall deserved you. But what did I know? I was a tomboy, into climbing trees and diving off rocks into the ocean. I understood nothing of what 'like' meant between a boy and a girl. I chewed on a nail while you watched me squirm away from your gaze.

You didn't laugh at me, just said quietly, 'I guess you're not ready for all that yet?'

I shook my head in disgust and you still didn't laugh.

'I didn't feel ready back then either. Kayla started dating when she was your age and I used to feel kind of left out.' You took a strand of my hair and combed the knot out of it with your fingers. 'I don't want it to be like that with us, Hannah. I want us always to be able to talk.'

You were about to go where I couldn't follow, into a world of giggles and whispers, lips brushing shyly for the first time. A world where manicures suddenly mattered and a whole bunch of stuff that I couldn't begin to imagine would become important. But your Jenny-like smile and kind hands reminded me that you'd always come back to this place to share what could only exist between the two of us.

You held out your little finger. 'Pinky swear!' And I crooked my little finger around yours. 'No boy will ever come between us,' you said and I grinned.

'No boy,' I promised back.

I never felt you'd leave me behind again after that. Just as when I was a toddler, trailing after you on stumpy, uncertain legs, and you'd wait for me to catch up when I needed you to. You'd always be my big sister and my closest friend in the world.

I open my eyes . . . and the world sucks again.

The clouds above me are perfectly white and puffy, clouds from a child's drawing in a blue sky. They look lower than they do back home, as if I could reach up and touch them. Like if I walked up the hills on that ridge over the lake, those clouds would brush my hair and leave it misted with droplets. I've never seen a sky look so close to earth. I can't decide if it's claustrophobic or amazing. I'm wondering what you thought of it. But then I don't know if you've ever lain here and looked. You're not a lie-alone-and-stare-at-the-clouds kind of girl. Always with people, always at ease with their noise, that's you.

'Rough day?'

The voice comes from above me and I twist my head round to find its source. I squint up into the sunlight and recognise the bartender from last night, the good-looking guy. Uncomfortable, I sit up. He has that scarily perfectly ruffled thing going on with his hair that only hot guys can pull off and I gauge he's somewhere around twenty to twenty-five. I feel suddenly flushed and twitchy – you would understand that, knowing me. To my surprise, he settles on the grass beside me.

'OK if I sit here?'

My natural retort would be, 'A bit late to ask now, since you already are,' but I hold back on that because his stop-in-your-tracks hotness has me flustered, so what he actually gets is a cautious, 'I guess.'

He laughs and I realise that it's the first proper laugh I've heard since they told us you were missing. 'You sound just like Jenny – your accent, I mean. Which is, doh, obvious, I suppose. Of course you do, but it surprised me somehow.' He laughs again, but this time at himself.

He mentions you casually, as if he doesn't know you're missing, but I know he does because of what he said last night.

'What's wrong?' he says, stopping as he sees the confusion on my face.

I shrug, unable to explain, plus this is a college-age guy and he makes me even more tongue-tied than guys usually do.

His face sobers. 'Unlike everyone else,' he says in a lower voice that's somehow so kind I feel even more shy of him, 'I'm not assuming something bad has happened to her.'

Now he has me interested, Jenny. I stop noticing that he's intimidatingly hot and all I care about is what he has to say.

'How well do you know Jenny?' And then as an afterthought, 'And who in hell are you anyway?'

He laughs again and it's kind of a nice laugh he has there. He holds his hand out for me to shake. 'I'm Tom. I work here, though I'm sure you've figured that out. How well do I know Jenny?' He shrugs. 'We get on quite well, I think.'

'Were you *seeing* her?'

He shakes his head. 'No, she's a lovely girl, but much too young for me. I'm between girlfriends and Jenny was on the rebound so we talked, as friends.'

You never mentioned a Tom. Is that because you thought I'd make assumptions?

'So why are you so sure she's OK?'

'I'm not sure. I just think it's likely. She's a bright girl, sensible too, and there's no reason to assume anything bad has happened to her.'

'Wait a minute! No reason? Nobody's heard from her in nearly a week. Jenny doesn't do that.'

He nods. 'I can see why you feel like that. Jenny told me you two are close. But I look at it like this – maybe she needs some space and disappearing is what she had to do to get that.'

This is crazy talk. 'Space? From us? She's a whole country away. How can she need space?'

'Not just from you – from everyone.' He sighed. 'I'm not explaining this very well.'

'Is this something Jenny told you?' I demand. 'Because if it is, why haven't you told the cops?'

'No, no.' He shakes his head vehemently. 'Look, I need to try to put this better. Jenny was having what you might call a time of discovery. She completely fell in love with England.'

That's true. You told me that yourself.

'She was changing how she thought about herself and she was trying to trace some of her English family. A guy who works here was helping her – he's into that stuff.' He hesitates. 'She was fairly mad with your mother for holding back on her about that.'

'Mom doesn't have any family left here.'

'What, none? Not even a distant cousin?' He screws up his pretty-boy face in disbelief. Put like that it does sound dumb.

'That's what Mom told us.'

'Well, Jenny didn't buy into that. Not one bit. It's possible that she may have gone looking for a relative. I don't know – maybe she thought she'd be back by now. Maybe she even found something out that made her really furious with your mother and she's taken off until she gets her head around it.'

'Jenny wouldn't do that!'

'I guess you know her best.' He shrugs. 'Maybe I'm overly optimistic, but that seems more logical to me. You know, you can go a little crazy when you're finding out who you are – I've been there. I suppose I thought I caught a few glimpses of Jenny in that place. Maybe – I don't know.' He looks at his watch. 'I'm sorry, I have to go. My shift starts in five minutes. I hope you get some good news soon.'

I try to swallow as he heads off back to the hotel, but my throat feels paralysed. He's wrong, isn't he, Jenny? You wouldn't do that to us. To me. But why didn't you tell me all that stuff about looking for Mom's family? I had no idea.

Is he right? Sometimes I get a flicker inside me of that craziness I think he meant. The desire to go and do something so not me that I scare myself, but it's there inside me like a burn – hot, demanding and painful when I don't answer it. And I don't even know what it wants.

Did you feel that? Is that what this is about? My good sister finally broke out and showed us all?

I've sent you six texts since I got your last message, all begging you to come back. I send you another now:

Please just tell me you're OK.

I hit Send and I pray to the God my grandma prays to in case He actually does listen.

CHAPTER 13

There's been no response to my text by dinner time. Mr Cadwallader joins us as we sit down to eat.

'Any news from the police?'

'Some possible sightings,' Dad answers. 'But they could be nothing. We were warned not to get our hopes up over every call that comes in.'

'But it could be something!'

'I'm hoping so. They're following up the information they received after the 6 p.m. appeal. More was coming in as I spoke to them and they'll call back later.'

Your boss smiles in relief. 'That sounds much more hopeful.' He turns to me. 'How are you holding up, Hannah?'

'OK. I was thinking I should speak to one of Jenny's friends here and see if she knows anything.'

'The police have already talked to all the staff, but you're most welcome to try. Who is it you want to talk to?'

'Cassie. Jenny said she works here as a maid.'

He looks blank for a moment and I realise just how many staff there must be. 'Oh yes, I know who you mean. My wife deals with the maids. I'll get her to arrange for you to meet her tomorrow morning. How's that?'

'That'd be great, thanks.'

He gets up with a smile. He's just grateful, I guess, to be able to do anything at all.

It's the impotence of waiting, Jenny, that rips its cat claws down your nerves. I get that now.

I check my phone again as I go to bed, but there's still no message from you. There's one from Mom though, letting me know she and Brandon love me. My eyes fill up a bit as I read it – a stupid, sentimental weakness that won't help anyone. I bury my face in the pillow until the sting goes away.

Dad's still waiting for a call from the cops. He said he'll come get me if there's any news. I'm so tired, Jenny, from all the waiting and hoping that I fall asleep before he does. Forgive me.

CHAPTER 14

I wake early. The first thing I do is reach for my phone, but there are no new messages and once again the day surrounds me with the heavy shroud of not-knowing. It's just getting light outside as I pull the thick drapes back from the window. My room faces out back from the hotel and behind is some woodland that stretches for what seems like miles. It's like a vacation snapshot – look, guys, here's where I stayed. How English is that?

I can't look away. If you were here by my side, you'd be staring in awe too. This view might have been the same for hundreds of years, history rolled out before me in a swathe of green. You used to ask me if I thought England would be as green as they say.

It is, isn't it?

I need to call Mom today. I need to hear her voice. I miss both of you so much.

Sleeping is best. Sleeping numbs everything. In my dreams you're not missing. In my dreams we're all home together again. But now I can't sleep. The stress of you being gone has intruded and woken me early to this faint misty dawn.

I feel the change as a sudden splinter of pain – I *hate* this place. I hate this country. I feel like I understand Mom now for hating England too. That's why I need to talk to her. Whatever happened, wherever you are, England's taken you away from us.

A figure comes across the expanse of grass and catches my attention. There's a mist rising up under his feet as the dew evaporates. I recognise him, even before I see the bird on his outstretched arm. It's the falconer boy. I can tell from the way he walks, unhurried but with a stride that could eat up miles and not tire. Something about that soothes my nerves just a little bit.

I curl up on the window seat among the heavy, heaped cushions to watch. The boy walks into the middle of the field and stops. From the way the bird's head tilts, he's talking to it. He pulls a covering off its head, like a tiny hood. I don't have any idea what kind of bird this is, a little hawk of some kind would be my best guess. I bet you would know, Jenny.

The bird shifts on his arm and he talks to it again. Then he flings his arm up and wide and the bird launches itself into the sky. The boy stands, watching it, his head thrown back. It flies for the trees and I clench my fists, wondering if this is a mistake and he's lost it. A high branch trembles as the bird settles on it. Through the old leaded glass of the window I catch the faintest of sounds – a whistle.

The bird soars back to his glove. He feeds it something, his head bent towards it, and it seems like he's whispering to it.

I draw back from the window. It's like I'm intruding on a private moment. I can feel the bond between them from here. I assume he flies these birds every day in the demonstrations, but he knows he's being watched then; he doesn't now and it feels wrong.

As I move back further, he launches the bird again and I stop. There's a hypnotic draw in watching its path into the sky and I just can't look away. I find myself pressed up to the window again to see better, despite myself. As I linger there, he casts the hawk off again in another direction and calls it back with that soft whistle. After a few times, as if this is only the most basic practice, he gets out a small object tied to a rope and, as the bird flies, he whirls the object round in the air. I squint – it looks like a small stuffed leather bag. The bird swoops on it and brings it down to the ground, tearing at it with its beak and gripping tight with powerful talons. It's then I realise what he's doing – he's teaching it to hunt.

I watch, fascinated, until he takes the bird away, loping off in that carefree stride over the field and around the side of the hotel.

I dimly recognise that I'm cold and shivering by the window. The sun's not risen enough to warm the room yet, so I scurry back to bed and dive under the covers. As my toes warm up again, the realisation comes that, for a few waking minutes, I forgot about you and was at peace.

Guilt crashes over me in a wave. That can't happen again. I can't be at peace until you're back with us.

CHAPTER 15

I keep checking this cellphone, Jenny, and you don't answer. If willpower alone could bring a message through, I'd have had a reply hours ago, but there's still nothing by the time I go downstairs to meet Cassie.

She's waiting for me in the coffee lounge. There are other guests and I look around for a moment, lost, until I see a girl in the far corner giving me a small wave. Of course she's recognised me. I'm too much your sister for her not to, albeit a smaller and darker version. Oddly, she's a little like you in that she's around the same height and slim with long blonde hair. If I saw her from behind, my heart might have leaped for a second in the hope that it was you, but from this angle there's no mistaking that her face is nothing like yours.

I don't know what to say when I go over to her. You would know, and you'd smile. I can't – my face is frozen into an off-putting frown. I can feel myself doing it, but I can't stop. The polite smile on her face fades quickly. This happens a lot with me. Never to you. But I guess there's not too much to smile about now anyway, is there?

'Hi,' says Cassie. She sounds nervous. Is that normal? I wonder if I should begin to be suspicious of everyone here. I mean, someone must know something about what happened or where you are, Jenny. I just have to figure out who and maybe Cassie is the answer.

'Hi,' I reply tonelessly and sit down.

We stare at each other and then look away, both uncomfortable.

'You wanted to talk to me about Jenny?' It's Cassie who's the first to find something to say.

I shrug. I look sullen, I know I do, but no one gives classes in how to interview strange girls about your missing sister and I don't know how to deal with this now I'm faced with it. I'm not like you – I can't just *talk* to people the way you can.

'Yeah.' And no other words come into my head. I sit there stupidly.

'I told the police everything I know,' Cassie says and I think she's going to go on, but a waiter interrupts and tells us we can have coffee on the house – orders of Mr Cadwallader. That seems to fluster her more than I do and I wonder why. Because she's a maid here? Is this some strange English thing that she can't accept a coffee from her boss while we're sitting here talking about you?

I'm caught looking at her like she's crazy. 'It feels weird. I mean, I've never even spoken to him,' she explains.

'How long have you worked here?'

'Just over a year. I'm having a gap year to earn money before I go to uni, so I started last June and I finish in September.'

'Like Jenny then.'

That seems to relax her and she sits back against the cushions. 'Yeah, except I started a few months earlier than her obviously.'

'Do you guys have lots in common then?'

'Quite a bit, yes. I'd just split up with someone too when she arrived so we were both single and . . .' she shrugged '. . . and not very happy about it at first. We talked about that and about other stuff too. Life plans, all that kind of thing, you know, and it turned out we got on really well.'

'Jenny talked about you more than she did anyone else. I figure you know her best here.'

The coffee comes and Cassie takes hers, still a little self-conscious. She reminds me of you in another way. Not about the coffee – you would never be uncomfortable about that – but she's easy to talk to in the same way you are. 'I can't stand doing nothing while Jenny is missing. Nobody seems to have a clue where she is so I have to try looking for her myself. Because one thing's for sure – I'm not leaving here until we find my sister.'

Cassie smiles. 'She said that about you, that you're very determined.'

I am. But determined comes with a price. It comes with awkward. It comes with not being at ease with people. It comes with loner, or it does when you're wearing it my way. Hey, maybe it always comes that way.

'She also said you two are very close.'

'Uh-huh, yes, we are. That's why I figured that if I spoke to her friends I might be able to pick up on some clue that nobody else has.'

Cassie nods with enthusiasm. 'If you could, that would be great because the police still don't seem to have found anything yet.'

'No, they haven't. They're following up some stuff from the appeal yesterday, but it all sounded vague. It's not like anyone called in saying, "Hey, she's right here," or anything like that.'

'Isn't there any news?' Cassie takes a sip of coffee.

'Just sightings from people who'd seen her out walking before. Nothing more.'

Cassie frowns. 'Did they say if she was alone?'

'I think so. Nobody mentioned seeing her with someone else. Why?'

'I've just been wondering over the past few days whether it's possible she could have been seeing someone she hadn't told me about.'

I sit up, alert. 'What makes you think that?'

'I'm not sure really. I mean, I'm not even sure I do think it. I just can't think of any other reason why she could have disappeared like this.'

'So, when you saw the cops, what did you tell them? So I understand from the beginning . . .'

'They wanted to know Jenny's routine,' Cassie says, screwing up her face as she remembers the exact conversation. 'So what I told them is that she normally helps get the kids up and has breakfast with them while Mrs Cadwallader bobs in and out to see them while she's getting ready. Then she spends the morning doing stuff with them and has lunch with them. Sometimes she takes them out for a walk, but if it's wet they don't go far. After lunch, she has the afternoon off and Mrs Cadwallader looks after the kids. Jenny likes to go for long walks then, even if it's bucketing down, and she's usually gone for a few hours. Sometimes we'd catch up with each other in the juice bar at the end of the afternoon before she went off to have tea with the kids. By dinner time, Mrs Cadwallader took over and put them to bed and Jenny was free. Sometimes Jenny would come round to my place in the evening.'

'Oh, you don't live here then?'

'No, I live in the village with my parents.'

'Do most of the staff live in or out?'

'Most of us are local so we live out. Only Jenny actually lives in the castle because she's in the Cadwalladers' wing near the kids. A few others live on the estate – some of them around the back in a converted mews block and others in cottages in the grounds.'

'So hardly anyone's here once you close up?'

'There's the night staff – porters, kitchen staff, bar staff – but they work on rotating shifts.'

'So once you go home for the evening, what does Jenny usually do?' I ask her.

'She has her own suite with a TV and chill-out space. But honestly I have no idea what she does when I'm not here. Once or twice we went to the pub in the village together, but she never mentioned going there with anyone other than me, sorry.'

'I guess if you live here you have your own friends to hang out with?'

'Not so much. They're all away at uni so I did spend a lot of time with Jenny, but I have to start here really early so late nights are a no-no. Mr and Mrs Cadwallader don't like to see staff yawning around the place. It gives the guests a bad impression.'

I frown. It all seems a bit insular. Practically feudal — everything seems to centre around Wolfscott.

'The Cadwalladers pay well,' she says, seeing my face. 'There are lots of worse jobs. Actually, around here there are practically no other jobs at all.'

'So did Jenny hang out with anyone else?'

'She talked to lots of people and she might grab a coffee with them, but I don't think there was anyone she hung out with any more than that. Or at least I thought so until this week.'

'So what did change your mind?'

'I don't really know. Maybe a couple of small things, like we seemed to spend a bit less time together over the last month than before. She seemed a bit preoccupied at times. Once, when we talked about the end of the season and me going away and her going home, she didn't seem like she was looking forward to it as much as she had before. Just little things that probably add up to nothing.'

Or they could add up to a whole lot.

CHAPTER 16

So I'm still no further on than I was before, Jenny. Cassie is going to think really hard about any other signs you might have given, little things you might have said that could mean you were seeing someone. We're going to meet up again tomorrow after she finishes work. I'm itching with impatience – that's a whole day. Another day without you makes it feel so much more serious. I really thought you'd be back with us by now.

I have to give Cassie time to think, I know that. Those words of hers keep revolving in my head, crashing off the sides of my skull – you didn't seem like you were looking forward to coming back home.

Was that what Mom was scared of when she didn't want you to come here? That you wouldn't want to come back?

I go find Dad to arrange a call for me on his cellphone. He has overseas for that and I need to talk to her real bad.

'Mom?'

'Hannah? Are you OK?'

'Yeah. We didn't find her yet, Mom – sorry.'

'I know, honey. Dad told me.'

'I wish she'd never come here. I'm so scared, Mom.'

'I know. We all are, baby, but you have to believe we'll find her.' Mom doesn't say it like she's managed to convince herself that she believes, but she's trying for me.

'It's so hard. It's like she's disappeared into space – nobody knows anything.' My voice is cracking, which is the last thing I should be letting happen, but it's my mom and at least there's no one else in the room. 'And sometimes I'm so mad at her because you didn't want her to go and if she'd listened to you we'd all be sitting round the table, eating dinner tonight. And this place is beautiful and amazing and all, but it's not home and I don't understand how she could want to leave us . . .'

Because I don't, Jenny. Maybe I'm just not as evolved as you yet. I can't imagine leaving home to go to college, let alone moving to a whole new country forever, because I'm wondering now if that's what you were thinking. And I don't get how you could do that to us at all. We need you. Our family has a hole in it without you – you're the happy, cheery, friendly one that everyone loves. If you're not there it'll never be right again.

Mom does the Mom thing – nothing said about my outpouring, nothing real, just lots of shush-shushes and baby-I-love-yous and it'll-all-be-OK-you'll-sees. But that stuff works from your mom, it really does.

'I wish I could be there with you, Hannah, truly I do.'

'How is Brandon?'

'He's OK. We saw a doctor today who is ninety-nine per cent sure that it's not the cancer back but some effects of the drugs he was on, so this new doctor wants to try something different. Brandon wants to try too.'

'Any risks?'

'Some, but nothing permanent so Brandon says he's got nothing to lose. Either he'll feel less sick or he won't. If he feels worse, he can stop taking the stuff and eventually it'll pass off. I don't know, honey. I'm going to talk to Dad tonight. I've got all the details written down to tell him – you know what I'm like, I just don't understand all that technical jargon.'

So Brandon has good news. At least there's that.

'You know what I keep thinking about?' Mom says as I'm just about to ring off. 'That time we took you to the fair cross state.'

When I hang up, I'm back there too, Jenny, in that memory with her.

I was six and you were eight. We'd been looking forward to that fair for weeks. I'd never seen anything so big in my life as those fields covered in every kind of fairground ride you could imagine. There were carousels with painted wooden horses, tracks with bumper cars, stalls to hook a duck or to take aim and throw a ball at a target that could win you candy or a giant cuddly toy. Our eyes were saucers of wonder as we looked around us and tried to figure out what to spend our few dollars on first.

Dad took us on a carousel ride first. I remember it so clearly: the wooden horse he lifted me on was called Maverick and the name was painted on his saddle. I pretended he was real as he swirled me round and up and down. After a few spins, I closed my eyes and we were riding alone over fields and hills, just me and my horse. When the ride stopped I didn't want to get off. Mom paid for me to go round again because she said she'd never seen me want to do something so much before. It was after that she took me to horseback riding lessons.

You wanted to try to win a cuddly gorilla next so you and Dad went to do that and me and Mom queued at the candy stall for rainbow-coloured gumballs. 'It's so bad for you,' Mom sighed as she handed over the money to the guy behind the counter.

I nodded and threw a handful of the little balls in my mouth and chewed until my cheeks were pouched out like a hamster. We ate hot dogs from a stall that afternoon, the first time Mom ever let us, and we slurped huge cups of sugary Coke down too.

I was kind of sleepy after all that fat and sugar and Dad

said definitely no whirligig rides for a while. It was you who chose the Hall of Mirrors to go in next. Mom sat on a bench holding our stuff while Dad took us in. We walked into a tunnel with mirrors at every kind of strange angle that made you fat, thin, funny-shaped, stretched out, squashed up. I laughed as you walked into one, confused and thinking it was a doorway because of the other mirrors placed around it, and then I did the selfsame thing on the other side of the corridor a moment later.

Dad and I found this cool rippled mirror that made us warp like waves of the sea as we walked towards it. We played around with that, laughing at each other for ages. At first you were there too, laughing along with us. I don't know how long it was before we realised you were gone. We thought you'd be just around the corner, but I guess we'd got disorientated in there and we ended up going back on ourselves a way before we worked it out and retraced our steps. It took us another forever to find our way out of the mirror maze and then we headed round to Mom waiting at the front, expecting to see you there. You weren't.

Mom got that slightly panicked look as she realised what had happened. Dad just shrugged. 'She'll still be in there. We've just missed her. I'll go back and look. Hannah, you wait here with Mom.' And he went back in.

Mom sat silent and tight-lipped, her eyes constantly scanning around, looking for you. She stood up to see better over the heads of the crowd and I sat on the bench, chewing my nails.

I hadn't been worried until I saw Mom's face, but now I could feel her fear and it awoke a wobble in my stomach.

But that was nothing to how white Mom went when Dad came back again without you, and how ashen his face had turned too. 'I don't think she's in there,' he said. 'She must have come out.'

'But where is she? She knew I was right here. Why didn't she come round to me?' She gripped his arm. 'Something's happened to her. Jenny wouldn't just wander off.'

'OK, we'll split up and look. Meet back here in ten minutes. If you see one of those lost kid points, check in with them and give her details.'

Mom grabbed my hand and towed me off in one direction, while Dad went in the other. We looked and looked for you, but after ten minutes' searching we hadn't found you.

'We're wasting time,' said Mom. 'You keep looking for her, David, and I'll go get help.'

She pulled me off through the crowd again, asking everyone she passed if they'd seen you and where the marshal's station was to report a missing kid. Eventually someone pointed out the way to her, but nobody had seen you. The marshal took your details and I waited by Mom's side as she wrote down your name and hers and Dad's cellphone numbers and your description.

And then I spotted you, a mop of bright hair through a parting in the crowd. A man had your hand and was pulling you the other way. You didn't look too happy, then you saw me too and reached out your other hand to me. The man gave you a sharp tug.

'Mom?'

She carried on writing, concentrating on filling the form in.

'Mommy?'

'Not now, Hannah, I need to do this.'

'But Mommy –'

'I said, not NOW!'

'THERE'S JENNY!'

That got her attention. She whirled round and scoured the crowd looking for you, following my pointing finger. But you'd gone, lost behind a sea of bodies.

'She was just there,' I whimpered.

You'd seen me. Why hadn't you come to us? Was that man trying to take you? My eyes narrowed. Have you ever seen a bull about to charge? I reckon that's what I looked like. I took off through that crowd like a Jenny-seeking missile, weaving through legs. Dimly I could hear Mom's voice calling to me as I ran, but nothing was stopping me.

As I reached you, you were pulling hard on the guy's hand. 'Please, I want my mom. She's back there. I saw her.'

He glanced down at you and gave you a look I really didn't like, before he carried on pulling you after him. All around the fairground, kids were arguing with parents over candy, over

73

rides, so no one paid your quiet protest a moment's attention.

I launched in on him with the hardest kick I could to his kneecap. 'YOU LEAVE MY SISTER ALONE, CREEP!'

They told me afterwards I went at him with the tenacity of a pit bull, kicking and punching at him and screaming my head off about how he was kidnapping my sister. Then Mom arrived and pulled me away.

An older lady who looked a lot like Grandma bent down and gave me a candy bar from her bag. 'That was real brave of you, sugar pie,' she said as Mom comforted you. The man was telling Mom you'd got lost and he was trying to find a marshal's station, but I didn't believe him. I chewed on the candy bar and held the old woman's hand until Dad arrived too. Her skin felt crinkly like tissue paper, just like Grandma's.

All of you were kind of shocked how batshit crazy I'd gone on the guy, especially as no one else seemed to think he'd been trying to take you, but I saw his face and I knew he'd been up to no good. Mom promised me a reward for being brave and I picked horseback riding. Which was totally awesome, but you know, Jenny, I was just doing the only thing I could. I never thought about it – I just did it. See, I didn't care if people looked or I was rude or nasty – not when I was mad as hell. That's another of the differences between us.

Do you remember that, Jenny? I'd still do that now. I *will* do that now.

CHAPTER 17

I walk slowly downstairs and out into the sunlight bathing the courtyard. There's a group of people gathered round the bird roosts. Curious, I wander over there and lurk at the back. There's a man in his thirties with an owl – even I recognise that – on his wrist and he's talking to the crowd.

'This is a snowy owl. He's called Bart and we've had him here at Wolfscott for six years. Bart is one of our display birds and we fly him most days. You'll be able to see him in action on the Falconer's Field behind the hotel after this talk. If anyone's not sure where that is, Harry here will take you round there.' He pointed to the boy I met on my first afternoon. So his name is Harry. It suits him.

Harry's face is impassive as the falconer goes on with his talk about the different birds they have, what they're fed on, their routines. I listen with half an ear. In all honesty, I would have been much more interested if I hadn't been so fascinated by how still Harry is standing. Silently unobtrusive, he's more of a distraction than if he'd been fidgeting around during the talk. He's as motionless as a statue and his face makes me wonder if he's listening or a thousand miles away from here in his head. I guess that wouldn't be a surprise. He must have heard this talk hundreds of times. So he's the apprentice to this guy maybe? He stands among the tethered birds and it strikes me he's more at home with them than the audience. Like the birds, there's nothing timid about his silence. It's as aloof as they are, the perfect self-possession that comes from utter disinterest.

I'll go watch the flight display after this. There's nothing else to do but wait for the cops to call back, until I meet Cassie again tomorrow.

A movement from Harry startles me as he takes the owl from the falconer with well-drilled ease, tethers it back to the post and then hands him another bird. He never makes eye contact with the man or the audience as he returns to his sentry position. I study his face. It's an interesting one: thin with sharp cheekbones, but broad enough to be strong – none of the weaselly look that some thin-faced boys have. His eyes are dark and could be grey or brown. His mouth is wider than average and the bottom lip is just a shade fuller than the top.

Overall, it's a face that I'd want to draw if I wasn't useless with a pencil, but you always said I had an artist's eye without the artist's hand; his face appeals to my eye. It's not conventionally good-looking, but it meets that standard in its own way.

There's a quiet that comes from shyness and a quiet that comes from just being still within yourself. I'm not sure which this boy is – maybe both and that's why it's hard to decide. He fetches another bird for the falconer with those calm, unhurried movements that I sort of envy.

That's it! That's what's interesting about him. I'd like that kind of . . . grace, I guess . . . myself. I always feel like I'm clumping around, lumpen and too solid, too anchored to the earth.

As he hands the bird over from his leather glove to the man's, his eyes catch mine and he flinches in recognition. I am not a welcome sight. This doesn't surprise me. I'm not often a welcome sight to any boy. I've learned to deal with that.

Do you remember my first day at high school?

We walked in together. You hadn't learned to drive yet and Dad gave us a lift to the end of the block. I was nervous, of course. High school was another world of cliques and making/breaking friendships and power play. I found all that tough enough to deal with in grade school and it was all about to step up to a whole new level.

'I was scared too,' you said as we walked up the steps to

the main doors. 'But you find your way around and everyone is really friendly because they all want to make friends too and they're as nervous as you.'

Yeah, Jacintha's little bitch clique from grade school – I bet they were totally nervous that morning. Would someone else be prettier than them? Must be terrifying, living life on the edge like that.

You showed me where the lockers were and where my homeroom was and then you waved goodbye. I was alone. There were some other kids in the room, but no one I knew from last year. I knew you would tell me to smile and say hi, but I just couldn't. I was about as capable of faking a smile when I was nervous as I was of making a manned mission to the moon.

'Hey,' a dark-haired boy said to me as I passed him in search of a seat where I might be inconspicuous. It was inconsequential, a nothing comment of greeting without meaning.

My brows snapped together and I glared.

Couldn't help it, Jenny. That's just how I am. I felt threatened, I guess, and I've never been able to work out how to stop that.

The effect is always the same though. The boy looked startled, then annoyed. He turned to the guy next to him as I walked on and whispered in a none-too-quiet voice, 'Wow, she's super friendly! What's her problem?'

And I wished I knew. I wished I could remake myself in your image so this would all be easier.

So why didn't I? Because there was always that cussed little part inside my heart that said, 'Damn them all to hell, I will be me and if they don't like me I'm fine with that.'

I guess that little part was big enough and cussed enough to win out. Little parts tend to be like that, ever noticed? They feel like the smallest, most hidden piece of you, but they seem to have the most power in the end.

Jacintha came in with a bunch of her followers, all hair-tossingly glossy and loud. Groomed, slim and perfect, which is how you had to be to join their club. Another girl I knew from last year slid in behind them and tried to make her way down the side of the room to the front.

Jacintha's head snapped round like she scented prey. 'Look, it's Elise. Hey, Elise.'

Elise turned round and muttered, 'Hey,' like she knew what was coming next.

Jacintha gave a sympathetic pout. 'The spots haven't cleared up? Too bad! You really should get your mom to take you to a good dermatologist.' She winced dramatically. 'Before that scars.'

Elise's mom worked two jobs after her dad left, just to make the payments on the rent. There would never be a good dermatologist for Elise and Jacintha knew that as well as I did.

'Thanks,' Elise replied quietly and sank into a chair at the front.

Jacintha smirked and a couple of her friends straight-out giggled. She was going to saunter up the room towards Elise when she saw me watching her. 'Oh hi, Hannah. Didn't see you there.' She looked around the room at some of the others beginning to take their seats. 'Made any new friends yet? Thought not. Weird how Jenny is so popular and you're so . . . different.' She smiled like poisoned honey, and with those words cursed me as a loner who no one would want to hang out with, because the others listened and heard and didn't know any better. And I didn't have the smarts to know how to fight someone like her then.

I'd do a better job now, but I've still not learned how to handle strange boys who say 'Hey' without acting like a total loser.

And right now I know I have that hostile look on my face that tells this boy, Harry, that I'm a loner freak.

Everyone starts to move off and I realise the talk is over and we're supposed to go to the field to watch the display. Harry looks at me sidelong as he passes, a medium-sized owl on the long leather glove he wears that goes right up his arm. I've never seen anyone have such a blank expression that you really have no idea what's going on behind their eyes. Most people give at least something away. I follow the small crowd, uncertain whether this is a good idea or not. It feels really dumb, but I guess I want to see what happens next. I feel a bit like a moth flying closer and closer to the light – like I'm drawn towards a danger I have no idea of.

Crazy, yes? I'm watching a bird display. What's wrong with me? Something sure is, but I don't know what yet and that's part of what keeps me following them to the display ground.

It's the falconer again who takes the lead and flies the hawk he's carried round there. Like when I watched Harry in that morning practice, the bird flies with the leather bag on the rope and the falconer tells us that's called a lure. He lets the bird go further out than Harry did and I wonder if that's his greater experience or the bird's. Some Americans at the front ask questions in between flights and the man answers them patiently, even though it sometimes makes the bird stir on his wrist as if it's impatient to be off again. Watching the hawk should be more impressive close up, but somehow I prefer the view from my hidden vantage point, looking down on the flight in the morning mist.

At the end of the display, Harry steps forwards and the falconer stands off to the side. 'Harry is now going to fly the barn owl for you,' he says. 'You'll see barn owls in flight during the day if you're lucky, but the best time to see them is at dusk. Their natural prey is voles and mice and shrews. Barn owls are nocturnal so measuring how many there are in the wild can be difficult, but since farmers have been given conservation grants to maintain their hedgerows that should help the population figures rise.'

Harry raises his fist slightly and the bird takes off, its pale golden wings catching the sunlight as it soars towards the trees. As it glides through the air on soft, silent wingbeats, Harry gives a whistle and the bird turns an arc to return to him. He holds out his fist, bait ready in his hand, and in a soft *whump* of closing wings, the owl lands.

'The barn owl normally swallows its prey whole. It then regurgitates any parts it can't digest, like fur or bones or feathers. The pellets can be found in the nesting and roosting sites where they build up in quite large quantities. You'll often see a barn owl at dusk on an exposed perch like a fence post because that's where they like to hunt from and where they'll wait to locate their prey. They've got exceptional hearing and can find their prey by sound alone, but they'll also hunt by flying low over the ground.'

The falconer nods to Harry again who casts the owl off once more. This time it's allowed to fly off to a high post at the far end of the field.

'Imagine you're a mouse. This is what you might see.'

Harry whistles to the owl again and it returns in that swift, silent flight, long and low over the grass, to land on his arm.

I swear the owl looks right at me then, and when I glance up, the bird boy is looking at me too with the same inscrutable expression. I turn away, my cheeks hot and uncomfortable, and leave the field, hurrying back to the courtyard. Behind me, the display is over and the crowd begins to break up.

As I scurry past the oak tree and head to the hotel door, a voice by my ear says, 'Any news yet?'

It's him. He's caught up with me in swift, silent strides like the flight of the bird still perched on his arm. He's more than a head taller than me and I have to crane my neck to look up at him as he's right by my side. I want to step away, but that would show weakness.

'No.'

'Oh. Sorry.' And he peels away from my determined route across the courtyard to return to the bird pens.

It's a curt response, even by my standards, but I cannot seem to act like a sane human person around boys. I should go after him, say something normal . . . Instead I slink back inside the hotel before I remember he's probably one of the people I should talk to further, ask some questions. Too late now.

It takes me a while to find Dad. He's in the coffee lounge and there's a horrible, hunted look on his face.

'What's wrong?'

'The police have decided that they're going to do a fingertip search of the route they think Jenny may have taken on the day she went missing. They've established a favourite walk from the contacts they've had in response to the appeal, but there are still no strong sightings on the day itself, so they want to go right over the area to look for possible evidence.'

'Evidence of what?'

His skin has taken on a greenish tinge under his tan, I notice distantly, as if he's someone else's father and not my own. 'Of anything. It's not looking good, Hannah. Nobody has seen her. The police think –'

'But the texts!'

'I know, but they still want to do this search. They say it's the next logical step in the investigation.'

I storm out and run up to my room. I need to be alone to process this. Not even in front of Dad can I bear this. I throw myself down on the bed, the pillows so soft that they rise up around my ears when I bury my face in them and drown out the sound of everything other than the hideous voices in my head.

They are looking for evidence of you. Of a dead you.

This is the first time I feel it could be true. That you could be gone, not just from our lives but from existence. How can that be true? How can someone as alive and beautiful as you stop *being*? A universe where that happens is impossible. It cannot be that a life simply stops, not a life like yours.

But it happens every day. Somewhere, every second, a life stops and loved ones cry bitter tears like I'm doing now. It feels so unreal though, like this is something that happens to other people, not to us. Even when Brandon was sick, I never believed he'd die. I was sure he'd stay with us. The same way I was sure when I got that first text that you're coming back to us.

I have to be right. I have to be.

If I'm not, the alternative is unthinkable.

CHAPTER 18

Dad's still in the coffee lounge with that sickly tinge to his skin when I finally go back down. 'When are they doing it?'

'It's scheduled for tomorrow morning. They're cordoning the area off now, but the actual search will begin at first light and they think it'll take most of the day.'

'But what will it tell them? If they find traces of fibres, things like that, they already know she used to go that way and those could have been left on any day she went up there.'

'They might find more than that.' Dad sinks his head into his hands and this is no longer the time or place to discuss this – too public. And I don't want to discuss it anyway. It's not happening. Not Happening At All.

So it comes to this. The cops are doing nothing to actually

get you back. They're assuming they're looking for a body, and you've stopped texting me, so I now need to move my ass and find some clues. Someone here knows something. I just have to figure out who.

Starting right back where I should have done two hours ago, I head out to the bird pens. There are some birds on the perches outside, but other than that it's deserted. I can't see Harry anywhere. After a slow walk around the courtyard, and then another, he still fails to show up and it finally occurs to me where he might be. I head out to the display ground and, sure enough, he's there with no audience as this isn't a display flight, but exercise for the birds, I guess. He has another kind of owl with him. If I thought the barn owl was big, this thing is massive.

'What's that?!'

He turns, not looking at all surprised by my snappy, abrupt question or even that I'm there. 'She's an eagle owl.'

'Oh.' Those dark eyes are too intense to be able to meet his gaze for long so I slide my eyes away to safety and look at the bird.

'It's one of the biggest species of owl in the world.'

'It's got a mean face.'

'So have you, but I won't hold it against you.'

I stare at him, open-mouthed, and watch the colour flush dull red up his face.

'Sorry. I shouldn't have said that.'

'Why not? It's true.' Because it is, and actually hearing it voiced turns out not to be the worst thing in the world. It's kind of freeing to hear it said right to my face, like I know we're not playing games.

'It's not, not really. I think I'd look mean if I had a sister I loved and she'd gone missing.'

He has a point there. I shrug and he lets the owl go. It heads straight for the nearest tree and settles there.

He laughs. 'She's so lazy. Finds the first possible perch every time. So is there any news?'

'No. They're going to do a fingertip search of the route she took on her walks most days. That's happening tomorrow.'

'Fingertip? Is that where they crawl along on their hands and knees looking for evidence?'

I've seen this on TV so I know. 'Yeah, they all line up together and they literally crawl over every inch of ground. It's going to take hours.'

'I saw some police vehicles going by the gate before. Wondered where they were going.'

'Probably to cordon the search area off. It's happening now.'

He nods. 'So it looks like they're not expecting good news then.' He's watching my face carefully as he says it.

I swallow hard, and again, and then a third time before I can get any words out. There's something weirdly sympathetic about a face that doesn't show any emotion, I realise, as he stands and watches me. 'No. I think they think she's dead now.'

'But you don't?'

'No.'

He smiles. 'You don't waste words, do you? No, no, that's not an insult. Not at all.'

'Do you think she's dead?'

He hesitates. 'I don't think it looks great. But you know her much better than me, so my opinion doesn't count.' He whistles. 'Got to get her back down before she nods off up there.'

The bird stirs, thinks about it and then another whistle brings her back down to his glove. I don't know how he keeps his arm still as she lands heavily – must be stronger than I suspected. The owl tears at a piece of meat in his glove.

'I thought, as the cops have given up on her, I should start trying to work out what's happened myself. I mean, if they think she's dead, they're going to stop looking for alternatives.'

'Maybe. But what did you have in mind?'

'Talking to anyone who knew her. Trying to piece together what she was doing and thinking when she went missing.'

'So that's why you're here talking to me, because you think I might know something?'

And then it hits me – I've been talking to this boy for, well, the length of a whole conversation and that just doesn't usually happen. 'Possibly. At least that's why I came out here to speak to you.' I shrug and look away into the trees. Somehow staring at green makes it easier to talk, ever noticed that? 'I'm not good at talking.'

'Me neither.' He strokes the bird and I watch the hypnotic movements of his fingers over her feathers.

'Why not?'

He screws his mouth up in distaste. 'Words mess things up. They don't come out right, don't say what you mean inside.' He smiles at the bird. 'She doesn't talk, but she makes me understand what she wants well enough.'

He has a smile that's like one of life's secret stashes – the squirrel's acorn haul for the winter, our candy box in the tree house, the flower bulbs that sit under rich soil waiting to bloom. A smile of hidden things of quiet pleasure.

'I don't hate words. I just don't like talking to people.'

'That's why you look mean, to put them off.'

For a moment, I'm stunned, then I counter. 'How do *you* put them off?'

'I pretend like I don't even notice them. And honestly, now, I mostly don't.'

I nod. This is a good strategy.

'I need to take this owl back. Want to come?' He asks hesitantly and it's a beautiful hesitancy with the wariness of wild, untamed things, and I do not understand, Jenny, why these thoughts even enter my head about a boy I don't know. I expect you could tell me and I miss you again, vinegar-in-cut sharp.

He sees me hesitate. 'It's OK,' he begins, to extricate us.

'I was thinking about my sister,' I say hurriedly. 'It hurt.' And I'm amazed I got those last two words out. They hang in the air, difficult and clumsy. But he nods.

We walk around to the bird pens in silence and he puts the eagle owl back in her cage. 'Ask me anything you want.'

'What do you know about her?' I ask him as he picks up what I now know is a goshawk.

'That she got to know practically everyone who works here while she's been living at the castle, which is not going to make your job any easier. She didn't seem to hang out with anyone too much except one of the maids — blonde girl, don't know her name. Everyone seemed to like your sister and the Cadwalladers were nice to her. And they can be a bit funny if they don't take to you. Especially Mrs C.'

He didn't say it as if he had any problems with them though, so I guess he gets on fine with them.

'She used to come and talk to Steve, the guy you just saw doing the public display. She was interested in the birds and sometimes she'd watch the displays if she was free or she'd bring the kids to see them. Sometimes she'd hang around for a bit, talking to us while we did stuff like this. Steve spoke to her more than I did.'

'Why?'

'I just didn't feel comfortable talking to her, even about the birds.' He bit his lip. 'She's not really from my world, you know.'

Yeah, I do know that. Me and this boy aren't citizens of your popular world, Jenny.

'Steve chatted to her though, lots. He liked how she was genuinely interested in the birds.' Harry rolls his eyes. 'Steve gets chatted up a lot by the girls here, even though he's married with two kids. Some of them seem to think that makes him a challenge. Jenny talked to him about his kids too though.'

'Yeah, she would. Was she seeing anyone, do you know?'

'I never saw her with a boyfriend. She used to go off a lot on her breaks, but I wouldn't know if she met someone then. That maid would know best.'

'Yeah, she doesn't. But she thinks Jenny may have been. I'm talking to her again tomorrow when she's had a chance to think it over properly.'

'Would Jenny not have told you?' He locks up the birdcages and comes out to sit on the rail beside me.

'I thought she would, but maybe I'm wrong about that.' I stop because I was going to tell him about what Tom the bartender said to me about you looking for family, and me not knowing anything about that — but that could be a mistake. I remember how Harry made me suspicious that first day, when

I had that feeling he knew more than he was telling. Just because I happen to find it easier to talk to this boy than I ever have before, I don't think that means I should be ignoring my gut when my sister's life could be at stake.

You still haven't texted me back. Maybe you're not OK. Not dead . . . not that. But maybe not OK. I need to be careful. Anyone here could be a suspect, including Harry.

'Did she ever mention her family?'

'Not to me. We only ever spoke about the birds though.'

'How? Can you tell me exactly?'

He sighs. 'I want to help you, but I don't think I can. It wasn't anything much at all. Just their names and what they ate and if one was a bit off colour she'd ask how they were. Honestly, there was nothing more.'

'How about what she said to Steve? You heard that, right?'

I could picture it – his silent presence getting on with the business of caring for the birds while my sister chattered brightly away to the other man. He wouldn't be able to help hearing even if he tried not to.

'She never said anything about a boyfriend, not that I heard.' He shuffles uncomfortably. 'Look, I don't know if she talked to him when I wasn't there. Maybe you'd be better off asking Steve.'

Dad comes out into the courtyard as I'm about to launch into another series of questions and he beckons me. 'I have to go, sorry.'

'OK.' Harry looks at his feet. 'Um, if you need someone to hang out with tomorrow while they're doing the search, I'll be in and out of here most of the day.'

'Oh, thanks!' I wasn't expecting that, not one bit. 'Uh yeah, might come over and, er, see the birds then. Could be a good distraction.'

'That's what I was thinking,' he says, still studying his feet.

'OK, yeah, then – thanks. See you around.' I scurry off to Dad before I say something stupid.

'Hey, honey,' Dad says as I reach him and he puts his arms round my shoulders. 'We need to talk to the police again. They're sending someone over.'

'Why?'

'I don't know. They're going to tell us when they get here.'

I tense into rigid attention. 'Like something awful?'

He shakes his head. 'No, but I think they may have found something out they need to discuss with us.'

We sit in the coffee lounge, waiting, and I'm learning every day how the worst kind of torture is the waiting and waiting for news about someone you love.

After an eternity, fed by so many offers of coffee from the waitress that I want to scream and throw things, Coombs arrives with another guy. He introduces him, but I don't take the name in and I don't care to ask again.

'So I'll get to the point,' Coombs says, looking at my face which feels bloodless. 'Something has come to light. We traced a bank account that was opened recently in the name of Cassandra Evans. She works here.'

'I met her this morning. She's a friend of Jenny's.'

'So it appears. We received a call from a bank clerk who recognised Jenny from the appeal. She told us that Jenny had been into the branch regularly to deposit money and had recently withdrawn a large sum. When she checked her records, that withdrawal was made the day before Jenny disappeared. But the account wasn't in Jenny's name.'

'It was in Cassie's?'

'Yes. We'll be talking to Cassie as soon as we can locate her.'

'But she was right here earlier!'

'She left early to go into town and she isn't back yet. We've got an officer waiting at her home. We've viewed CCTV from the bank though and we are convinced the girl in the footage is Jenny.'

'They do look kind of alike from the back. Even I thought that.'

'Can we see it?' Dad asks.

'I suggest you come over to the station in the morning and take a look. That will confirm the matter for us and also give us chance to speak to Cassandra Evans.'

'I don't know why Jenny would use another bank account

though,' Dad says. 'She has her own back home. She could have deposited into that.'

Because there's something you didn't want us to know. That's what we're all thinking right now. Jenny, what is going on?

CHAPTER 19

Dinner is awful. It shouldn't be, but I have no stomach for it. I just need to see you again. I need for all this to go away. As soon as we're done pretending to eat, I make excuses and sneak outside. There's a bench in the dark out beyond the courtyard and the lights from the castle where I can sit and watch the moon. I need fresh air.

Crazy, because what the cops told us wasn't bad news. It looks like you could be OK. Like maybe this was all part of some plan.

It's been like riding a rollercoaster today. First Cassie with her idea that you were seeing someone, then the cops acting like you're dead, and now you're using a fake bank account and what the hell does that mean?

I'm all over the place with this and I don't know where to turn next. I should be inside with Dad, but I don't know how. He looks so ripped apart by all of this. I can't deal with it myself. He's going to call Mom. I want to talk to her too, but I'm trying to give him some time with her so I'll speak to her later.

'Are you all right out here?' a voice says through the darkness and I hear the crunch of gravel as feet step off the grass on to the path.

'Who is it?'

'Tom, from the bar. Remember?'

I relax. 'Yeah, I remember. I'm OK. Just been a heavy day.'

He sits down beside me, hands clasped on his knees. 'It must be very difficult for you. I can't imagine how I'd cope in your shoes.'

'It's hard, yeah.'

'You have to stay positive. Jenny would want you to, wouldn't she?'

'I guess. Like I said, been hard today though.'

'Why?' His voice is so kind, so calm.

'They're doing a search of where Jenny goes walking tomorrow and it's like they're expecting bad news. But I spoke to Cassie this morning and she told me she thought Jenny might be seeing someone and then the cops came and —' I stop because I shouldn't be telling him this at all.

He nods. 'And you don't know what to think. Of course you don't. Listen, whatever reason Jenny has for leaving like this, she wouldn't want you to be hurt by it. I know her well enough to be sure of that. You have to trust that this will work out. How come your mum isn't here?'

'My little brother is sick and she has to stay home with him.'

'I bet you wish she was here.'

'Yeah, I do. She didn't want Jenny to come here in the first place. I wish she'd listened to Mom now.'

'Why was that?'

'Mom hates England. She left when she was old enough and moved to the US. She wanted Jenny to stay home.'

'Hmm.'

'Didn't Jenny tell you that?'

'Yes, I just wondered what your take on it was, that's all.'

'What did Jenny say about it?'

'Pretty much what you did. And that she wanted to find out more about her English family who she was convinced must exist. But I think I told you that already.'

Is that what happened, Jenny? You found them and you withdrew that money so you could disappear and do . . . what? I'm not convinced that makes sense. I can't buy you were too scared of Mom to be open about it. You came here after all. Or did you find out something bad?

I slam my hand on the bench, hard enough to ache right

up my arm. The pain is a welcome distraction.

'What's wrong?' Tom's soft voice asks.

'I hate the not knowing!'

'For what it's worth, I hate it too. I'm worried about her. I wish she'd get in touch so we knew she was OK.'

'I forget her friends feel that way too. I feel kind of selfish now.'

He puts his arm round me. I go absolutely rigid with shock, but he doesn't appear to notice and squeezes my shoulders gently. 'You're her sister and you're entitled to be selfish at a time like this. It's up to her friends to support you. Maybe you should get some sleep. It sounds like tomorrow could be another tough day.'

I get up, escaping from the circle of his arm before he realises how uncomfortable I am there. 'Yeah, thanks. You're right. I'll do that.'

'Take my number in case you ever need to talk to me – here, I'll call your phone so you have it.' He taps my number in as I reel it off and then my phone rings. 'There, now you have someone to call if you need a friend.'

I can't help but smile back at him. He looks so concerned for me behind his smile that I feel I have to make the effort to seem comforted. There's something about his kindness that kind of pulls that response out of me.

I walk back up to my room. I'll go say goodnight to Dad and

give Mom a call, but Tom's right – I'm tired out, especially after waking at dawn. I need some sleep to get some perspective on all of this. I just wish there was someone I could talk to without having to guard what I'm saying all the time.

That's the trouble. Up until now that person's always been you, Jenny.

CHAPTER 20

Sleep came as soon as I laid my head on the pillow. But once the first part of the night was done, it evaded me again and I woke to darkness and the sound of my own thoughts. No matter how I replayed all the events of the last few days, I couldn't get them to make any more sense than they had the night before.

At dawn, I'm waiting at the window in pyjama bottoms and a sweatshirt and thick socks. Harry appears in the early light as he did yesterday with a bird on his arm, the same one I think. He lopes across the grass. I have this wild urge to go down there and sit on the fence in the cool morning light, with the mist dampening my sweatshirt, and watch the bird swoop and soar. To hear the fluffle of feathered wings through the air, and to listen to Harry's silence.

Before I know what I'm doing, I'm closing the door of my room behind me and hurrying downstairs. Because this might be the only moment of peace I have today and rationalising my thoughts is not what I want to do right now. Because maybe it's time to act differently to how I've always acted before.

I don't know – something inside me says 'Do this' and I just obey.

My feet are wet before I've gone ten steps over the grass, dew soaking through the fabric of my sneakers. They're sodden by the time Harry sees me. I don't go up to him, but skirt around to the fence and hoist myself up to sit on the top rail. He waves a silent acknowledgement and I think he looks pleased for a moment. I watch him fly the hawk.

It's like a dance between the two of them, the release, the recall, the return, all perfectly matched and in time. They both know their parts and perform with a grace that takes my breath away. There's no sound out here but the song of tiny birds from the woods behind me and the hawk's wings and Harry's whistle. This is how morning should always sound. I understand now why some people love to wake early. Before the world's noise starts, life makes so much more sense. Out here, I am calm. Out here, I know you will be found and I just need to keep faith. Out here, there is me and this boy and the bird and we start to understand each other. As I watch, I learn the bird's flight as Harry must have learned it in the beginning.

The way it turns in the air, the angle it will take as it returns to the glove, they begin to be familiar to me.

It's the same when I'm out on a horse on a trail back home: the horse and me and the sun in the sky and that stillness inside I can never find when I'm surrounded by people. It's only in that stillness that I know who I truly am.

I've lost track of time when Harry waves at me to come over. I slip off the rail and squelch through the grass. My feet are chilled inside my wet sneakers, but that doesn't matter at all.

'Do you want to fly him?' he asks.

'I-I-I could?' I squeak. 'I don't know how.'

'It's OK, I'll show you.' He slips the glove from his hand, somehow holding the bird further up his arm without getting clawed. 'Put this gauntlet on.'

I pull it on. It's too big for my hand, but I'll manage.

'Here,' he says, settling the hawk gently on to my glove. 'He knows what to do. You just need to follow my instructions. Let me take charge of your arm.' And he wraps his fingers around my arm, just above where the bird is sitting.

It is the most personal thing I have ever felt. A total invasion of me. I can smell him, a lingering scent of woodsmoke and leather and soap. It makes me dizzy and I don't know why that should be. All the tiny hairs on my neck stand up, but not in fear. It's as if they recognise something I don't. His fingers rest on my thick sleeve, but I can feel their gentle pressure and the strength in them. My heart beats so fast that I want to sit down to escape from the intensity of this feeling, whatever it is.

'And release him,' he whispers in my ear, a warm breath that sends shivers down my neck as surely as if he'd kissed me. He jerks my hand upwards ever so slightly and the hawk flies. 'There, you did it.'

I'm shaking. Can he feel that?

He steps away a little and, despite what I just thought, I want him back close again. I don't know what this is, why this is.

We watch the hawk fly, side by side.

'He's beautiful, isn't he?' he says with pride.

'Yes. Why do you always bring him out so early in the morning?'

'He's my own bird, not Wolfscott's, so I fly him before I start work.'

'Oh! I didn't realise he wasn't one of the display birds.'

'I'm training him for that eventually. When I strike out on my own, he'll be my main demonstration bird, but for now he gets to be just a hunter. He finds his own meat and he comes back because we're a team.' He whistles and takes my arm again.

Him being close again, it's the danger in the lightning storm and the thrill of the pounding rain and the utter at-oneness that is being out there in middle of all of that, all those things at once. He holds my hand in position as the hawk flies back in. And all at once, from nowhere and for no reason I can explain even to myself, I am in love. I have the most lunatic insanity in my head – that now and forever this is where I want to be, who I want to be and who I want to be with.

I laugh at the notion of Insta-Love, you know that. I hate it in books. It's so fake. But oh my, it is *real* and it's happening to me now. I don't even know Harry, but at the same time I know him better than any boy I have ever met. There is something inside us that is sparked from the same fire.

The hawk lands, and with it the knowledge that nothing about me will ever be the same again. I dare, I don't know how, to look up at him and he's staring at me open-mouthed as if he feels the same too. His eyes are brown with grey flecks, like hazel twigs. He reaches down and I know what's going to happen and I don't believe it all at once. His lips brush mine, soft as the hawk's wings.

It's a moment I never thought would happen, not to me. Not with anyone.

He leaps back as if I burned him, grabs the hawk from me and breaks into a trot away down the field.

I stand there, trembling, and I don't call him back, but watch as he vanishes around the side of the castle. I'm still wearing his glove and I slide it shakily off my hand.

Cassie isn't in the coffee lounge when she said she'd be. I ask at the counter if anyone has seen her, but they shrug so I go to reception and ask there. The woman says she'll go find out. It takes her a long time to come back, but when she does it's to tell me that Cassie didn't turn up for work this morning. I hover uncertainly then. I don't want to go out into the courtyard in case Harry is there. In the end, I go back up to my room.

Dad is in his room doing some work on his computer. He has to, he said, to keep his mind off things. There's nothing to do but lie on my bed and stare at the ceiling and think. And that's the last thing I want to do right now.

I should be thinking about you. Now Cassie hasn't turned up I'm no further on than I was yesterday night. She could be at the police station, I guess. We'll find out later when the cops come round.

What I shouldn't be daydreaming about, but I can't stop myself spinning round and round in my head, is Harry. My first kiss. I still don't know how it happened. It was like I was drunk. Did I do it wrong? Is that why he ran off? Or perhaps he ran off because it was a mistake.

Do you know what – I can't even get a kiss right and there's me thinking I love him. I'm so dumb – you can't love someone just like that. *Stupid, stupid girl!*

I'm so busy yelling at myself in my head that I hardly hear the soft knock on the door. It takes a second knock for me to be sure. I pad over the floorboards in bare feet and crack the heavy wooden door open.

Harry's standing there, glancing down the corridor. 'I'm

not supposed to be up here,' he mumbles.

Some braver-than-usual part of me grabs his sleeve and pulls him inside. The bravery doesn't last long. As soon as I've dragged him in, I retreat.

'I came to say sorry,' he says, staring at his feet, which I'm coming to realise is a habit. 'I'm sorry it's taken me so long but it took me until now to think of what to say.'

He's going to confirm all my worst fears and my heart is going to be broken before it even has a chance to understand what is happening to it.

'I didn't know what to say. That's why I ran off. I've . . . I've never kissed a girl before.'

Oh. My. God. I did not expect that. Obviously he's a quiet guy, but he's about seventeen and he's, well, beautiful!

'It was my first kiss too,' I say in a rush.

He screws his face up. 'What? No way. You're just saying that to be nice.'

'I'm never nice. And I'm shocked, for the record.'

He sort of laughs. 'I told you, I'm not good at talking. And girls like talking. They like the patter, don't they, and I'm useless at it.'

'Not all girls.' Some girls like the quiet ones who don't have to fill every second with how great they are. And those girls might not even know they like that until they meet someone like Harry.

'What about you?' He looks directly at me with those amazing eyes, eyes that would keep my secrets forever, they tell me.

It's difficult, but I try to explain. 'Loads of guys, all they want to tell you is stuff to impress you, not anything real or true. It's like there's nothing more to them than . . . advertising blurb. Nothing genuine. If you looked behind the gloss, there'd be nothing.'

'And you don't want that?'

'No, I don't want that. I don't even like guys like that. I don't want a fake.' And that's true. I only found that out this very second, but it's true. All this time I've been seeing these guys and thinking there was something wrong and awkward with me for not being into them or able to communicate with them. Turns out they're simply not what I want.

He takes a deep, shuddering breath and his eyes burn with something I don't recognise. 'You have no idea what you just said,' he says, his voice shaking.

A knock at the door makes us both jump.

'Hell! I can't get caught here!'

'Hide in the bathroom!' I shove him in there and then go to answer the door.

It's Dad. 'The police are here,' he says grimly.

CHAPTER 21

I know it's serious when Dad takes me to a private room. They don't want to risk anyone overhearing, he says.

Coombs is wearing a stern face. 'As you know, we've been trying to catch up with Cassie Evans to explain what's going on with the bank account held in her name that we think Jenny has been using. Cassie was expected home last night after a trip into town. She never returned. Her mother has reported her missing.'

'Do you think she's with Jenny?' Dad asks.

'We don't know. Her disappearance could be completely unrelated, but obviously the weight of evidence at the moment would suggest not. We have considered the possibility that our conversation about her was overheard by a member of staff here and she's been tipped off. She may have run away to avoid having to speak to us. Or we may have a more serious problem on our hands.'

'You mean whoever has Jenny has her?'

'We just don't know, Mr Tooley. The only thing we can be sure of is that we have CCTV of a girl who may be Jenny. I'd like you to come down to the station now and make an identification, if that's all right.'

'Of course. Has the fingertip search started?'

'Yes, it has.'

'Hannah, honey, do you want to come with me or stay here?'

'I'll come. I just need to grab my jacket from my room.'

I speed off upstairs, but Harry has exited the bathroom, hopefully without being seen. I get my jacket and descend the stairs at a slower rate. I don't like this new development, not one bit. It makes my skin crawl with nerves for you.

Down at the station, with a plastic cup of weak coffee, we watch the CCTV. 'This is the first occasion,' says Coombs. And we see a girl with long hair come into view and take her place in line. Dad and I sit forwards immediately.

'That's her! That's Jenny!' he says.

'You're sure?'

'No doubt at all. It's Jenny.'

'That's interesting. This footage is dated a couple of months ago. If you watch the rest of this clip, you'll see she goes in here and opens an account in the name of Cassandra Evans, with all the necessary documentation, and deposits several hundred pounds.'

'Where did she get that money from?'

'We'll need to contact her bank in the US and see if she put her pay in there as you said she had or if she's saved some up and deposited it in this account instead.'

We watch you on the footage, the first time we've seen you since you disappeared, and we are greedy for it.

'She appears in the branch several times over the next few weeks, depositing smaller amounts. Again, I'd like you to confirm that each sighting is Jenny.'

He shows us each clip in turn. They are all you, with your bright hair and soft smile to the teller. It makes me wonder how I could have thought you'd changed when here you are, just as I know you.

'And this is the last one, the day before she disappeared. She withdraws a substantial amount from the account.'

There you are, coming into the bank, shaking rain from your hair and your umbrella. I look for signs of stress, but I see none. You look the same as ever, tapping your foot to the music playing on your headphones as you stand in line. You go to the window and talk to the bank teller and you're smiling. There's a long pause while you sign things and the teller goes off to get the money. You put it away inside your bag and then you leave. And –

'Whoa, did you see that?' I point at the screen.

'See what, honey?' Dad asks.

'There, at the end, as it switches cameras. Can you rewind that part again?'

Coombs nods to the techy guy who gets on it. 'What did you see?' he asks me.

'I want to be sure. You should look for yourselves and see if you spot it in case I'm mistaken.'

'OK, have we got it yet, Jack? Yup, here we go then.'

We all watch, leaning towards the screen as you tuck the money away then stroll out of the bank. You go down the steps, one, two, and you smile and speak . . . to someone just out of sight . . . and then the film cuts out.

'My God!' says Coombs and it's the first time I've seen him shaken. 'You're right. Someone else is there.'

'But we can't see them!'

'Not on this footage we can't, but there's CCTV in the town and we may be able to pick them up on that. I'll get the team straight on it.'

A lead. At last there might be a real lead. If we can find out who you were with, maybe it's not hopeless after all.

'Is there any news yet from the search?' Dad asks, his hands knotted in his lap. We're all tense with a hope that didn't exist a few minutes ago.

'No specifics. Which is not necessarily a bad thing. In a way, we don't want to find anything as it's not likely to be good news. A lead like this one here is much more promising.'

'So what are you really looking for out there?' I ask. 'Blood, human remains, signs she was dragged off or killed? Is that it? You're searching for evidence of her death. Well, you can see here that my sister could be alive. Why don't you concentrate as much effort on looking for a living Jenny as a dead one? If you did, she might be back with us by now.'

'We are keeping our minds open to a number of possibilities,' Coombs replies, masking the expression he wants to have with a bland, professional detachment.

'Oh yeah? So if you really believed she could be alive, why did it take me watching that film to spot she's with someone? Why didn't you see it yourselves? Because you're not looking for it, that's why!'

'That's enough, Hannah!' Dad grabs my shoulder and shakes me.

'No, no,' says Coombs, looking me straight in the eyes. 'No, she's absolutely right.'

CHAPTER 22

Mr Cadwallader sends a car to bring us back to Wolfscott. He thought it would be more comfortable for us than the police car. The search is still in progress and we have to pass through a police blockade to get back to the hotel. The car pulls up at the main doors. When we get out, I can see Harry over by the birdcages. He's standing, watching us, with an owl on his arm.

'Dad, I just need to go talk to someone. I'll be up later.'

Harry turns away when he sees me coming over and heads into the cage block, but when I get closer, it's clear he's waiting for me, not avoiding me. I slip inside the wire-mesh door. We're still visible if anyone gets up close, but it feels less exposed to prying eyes in here.

'We had to go to the police station. They have some

CCTV of Jenny they wanted to show us.'

'To ID her?' Harry asks as he puts the owl back.

'Yeah. There's one bit that looks as if she was with someone. They don't know who, but they're going to go through the CCTV in town and see if they can pick anything up there. But that could take a while.'

'I suppose it could be anyone – a friend or something. Any news from the search yet?'

'No, but they say that's good.'

He closes the door on the owl and turns to me. 'I've got some free time. Do you, er, want to do something?'

'Sure. I'm on sitting-around-here-and-waiting duty again otherwise. What did you have in mind?'

He looks at his feet. 'I have absolutely no idea,' he confesses. 'I've been trying to think of something for the last hour, but I've still not come up with anything.'

I laugh. His honesty is refreshing. 'We could go for a walk. I don't know any places round here. You could show me somewhere good.'

'You like walking?'

'Sure I do. Me and Jenny used to do some trekking together back home.'

He brightens. 'Oh, OK, I think I do know somewhere then.'

He leads me out of the courtyard and over the drawbridge. I pause to admire the moat. 'It kills me there's a moat. It's the most English thing ever.'

Harry sniffs. 'It's a bit of a nuisance really. Has to have algae cleared off it every summer. Still, the ducks like it.'

I'm enchanted by his complete lack of interest. 'You see, that's because you're English and it's so much a part of over here that you're not blown away by it.'

He gives me a sidelong look of amusement. 'You think? So if I went over to America, what would blow me away there?'

I contemplate it as we head off through the woods. 'I guess maybe the Rockies or somewhere like that. The wildlife there is incredible. We went this one year on vacation and it was just the best experience. Dad keeps wanting to go back. I know they have bald eagles there – you'd want to see them.'

'Yes, I would. That'd be cool.' His smile surprises me. I've never had a boy look genuinely interested in what I have to say. Of course, you might say that's because I don't generally talk to them and I couldn't argue that point.

'Where are we going then?' Our route is lined with pine trees and the scent of the resin in the air around us has me sniffing with pleasure.

He's looking down at me and he sniffs too. 'It does smell good.'

'Like Christmas. I love Christmas. Do you?'

The smile fades. 'Not that much,' he says and then points off down a path to our right. 'We're going that way. It brings us out at a mere. It's pretty there, if you don't mind a longish walk.'

'No, I don't mind that.' I'm still entranced by being with a boy I can talk to. Some of me wants to cut and run before it all goes wrong. But more of me is fascinated by the feeling of being with him. Even the way my pulse skitters when he looks at me feels good. 'But what's a mere?'

'A shallow lake. There's a lot of them in this area. This one doesn't have many visitors as it's on private land so you wouldn't normally get to see it if you were a tourist.'

'Awesome.' Although it does occur to me that walking out to a remote lake with a boy I hardly know isn't something my dad would appreciate.

We spend much of the walk in silence. He stops a couple of times to point out something in the trees above – a woodpecker once, and then a baby squirrel and its mom. When we reach the lake's edge, I gasp. It really is beautiful. There's a pebbly shore where we stand, but the rest of the lake is surrounded by reeds. It's a long expanse of water shining silver under the sun. A heron takes flight past us. There's a large boulder by the water's edge and Harry perches on it. There's room for me so I sit next to him.

'I come here when I need to . . .' He shrugs. '. . . Just be myself, I suppose.'

'I get that.'

We sit together and watch the birds on the water. There's no need to talk. I am absolutely comfortable listening to the sounds of water on shale and birdsong. Harry seems like he's really comfortable with that too.

It's so peaceful here, surrounded by the trees. My skin feels clean when I'm in places like this. I tell Harry that, just out of the blue. He turns to me and his eyes register his amazement.

'Do you feel like that too?' I ask.

'Yes, but I could never say it like that.'

I have to smile at him. 'You don't need to say it. You sort of . . . ooze it!'

He lets out a laugh. It's not really that loud, but it echoes in the quiet around us. 'Nice!' Then his eyes duck away from me and he puts his fingers over mine where they rest on the rock. 'You've got tiny hands,' he says.

'The rest of me isn't exactly big.'

'No,' and he says it like it's a good thing.

He lifts my fingers to his mouth and kisses them softly. How did this boy know that to take my hand in a place like this and kiss it would so totally overcome me? Maybe he doesn't know. Maybe we just . . . fit.

I take courage and stroke his fingers with mine and it feels like the most natural thing ever. When he leans over and kisses my lips, he pauses before our lips meet. He waits for me to pull back. When I don't, he gives the tiniest of sighs – a sigh of relief – and sinks into the kiss.

We're both still figuring out how this works, but it doesn't matter. It doesn't matter if our noses bump or our teeth clash or we don't quite synch our heads the right way. What matters is that this feels so good, even with our mistakes, and that neither of us care if we screw up. I can feel in his kiss that he doesn't mind at all when I do.

It's the most liberating thing in the world. After all the worrying you do over your first kiss, and all you hear from other people about how it goes wrong and the boy never talks to you again, or worse tells everyone and they all laugh at you, then you meet someone and all of that is just garbage. Because when you kiss him, it's all OK. Even the bits that go wrong.

When we stop, he doesn't pull away completely. He's still leaning close, looking right into my eyes. He doesn't know what to say, but that's OK because I don't either.

But I need to get back or Dad might worry. When I stand up, I keep hold of Harry's hand. We walk back together, our fingers intertwined.

I didn't know it was possible to feel so right with myself.

I'm getting ready for bed when your text arrives.

I'm OK. Don't worry. I found something important out.

I text back immediately.

What are you talking about? Where are you? Everyone here is scared as hell for you. Please come back.

You found something important out. What can be so important that it makes you put us all through this? I wait for a return text. But there isn't one. After an hour of sitting, staring at my phone, I give up and go to bed. I'm going to tell Dad and the cops in the morning. I feel like if I do it now I might jinx things and you won't text back. Maybe if I trust in you and wait, you will. Maybe.

I toss and turn on the pillow, trying to find a cool spot for my tormented head. And now I have another problem, like I didn't have enough with you: Harry.

I always thought you'd be around to talk to if I ever got to falling in love. In my head, I always imagined turning to you, like I do over everything else. For guidance, just to share with – you've always been there.

Here's the thing. When I'm with him, it feels so easy and right. But at times like now, when I'm on my own, the doubts set in again. Doubts that make me think I'll blow it or that I'm reading him wrong. And I want to ask you if this is how it always is with boys or whether it's me being a freak again. Who can you ask those questions to but your sister? So you have to come back, Jenny, because I need you.

I think I'm making the most dumb-ass mistake here. I'm falling in love with a boy who lives an ocean away and pretty soon we'll be going back home and he'll be here. Only I could be so stupid. There's the whole of America and I fall for an English boy. It's as if I like to make my life more difficult than it has to be.

It's his eyes, Jenny. They're the stillness of the forest, the quiet of the lake, the freedom of wild things. Nobody tells you in a dumb teen magazine how to protect yourself against a boy with eyes like that. They don't even tell you boys like that exist. How was I supposed to stop this from happening?

The bad thing is I don't want to stop it happening. Right in the middle of the nightmare of losing you, someone came along that I thought could only exist in a dream. These are the worst and best days of my life all in one.

Just come back now, please.

CHAPTER 23

There's no text in the morning and when I trudge through to show Dad before we go down to breakfast, he explodes at me for not telling him last night and calls the cops straight away.

I'm going to be honest with you, Jenny – we're all breathing easier after that message, but we're really frustrated too. In fact, Dad's pretty mad with you right now.

'What the hell has gotten into her?' he yells when he reads the message. 'She's found out something important! What's that supposed to mean? She'll find out something a lot more important when I see her and that's about how to treat the people who love her.' Most of his anger is the relief of you not being dead. He throws my phone on to the bed. 'I really don't know what has come over her. Your mom was right – we

123

should never have let her come here.'

He looks tired, even after a night's sleep. I've been up since dawn. I went to watch Harry training the hawk. It's called Merlin, he told me. I feel kind of peaceful from the early start in the soft morning light and watching the hawk in flight. Harry gives me his cellphone number, but he warns me it's often turned off in the day because the ringing upsets the birds. 'If you need to leave me a message to meet you on my break or something,' he says gruffly, 'you can always put one on the cage door. I'll see it there.'

I'm glowing that he wants to meet me enough to tell me that.

At breakfast I chew on some fried bacon and miss you like toothache. In a way, you have given me some advice over Harry. I'd just forgotten. At least it wasn't over Harry at the time, but looking back it fits.

We were in the tree house, of course. One of your friends had told you her little brother was interested in me.

'So?' you said, raising a questioning eyebrow at me.

'So what?' I picked at a scab on my knee where I'd skinned it climbing a tree with Brandon the week before.

You frowned at me. 'You know that's gross, right? So Kyle likes you, is what. You complain that boys don't like you and now here's one that does.'

'I don't complain. I just say,' I replied sulkily. 'You talk to me about boys and I make a valid point. How is that complaining?'

You rolled your eyes. 'OK, but it doesn't change the fact that Kyle likes you and you're trying to duck the issue.'

'Kyle doesn't even know me.'

You put your arm around my shoulder. 'Hannah, he doesn't need to know you. Not yet. He's attracted to you.'

'Well, I don't know him.'

With infinite patience, you tried again. 'Don't you think he's cute?'

I kicked my feet against the wall of the tree house, listening to the thud of sneaker soles on wood. They made a satisfying *thwump*. 'I don't think he's anything. I don't know him.'

You shifted your hand to stroke my hair, perhaps to stroke the knottiness out of me. 'So what you're saying is you need to know a boy to get interested?'

'I don't know. Maybe.'

You pursed your lips. 'Do you have a picture in your head of a boy you'd think *was* cute?'

'Nope.'

'You're not being very helpful here. If you don't like Kyle, that's OK, but are you giving him a chance? He might be really nice.'

I kicked the wall again, scuffing my heels up and down it. 'I don't want to see if I can get to like someone. I want to like them, period. Not somehow make myself do it. Is that really how it's supposed to work? Is that how it works for you? You go out with a guy you haven't even noticed exists and you see if you can make yourself get into him because nobody else is interested in you?'

'Oh, Hannah, no! No, that's not what I meant.'

'Then what did you mean, because that's how it sounds to me?'

You sighed and stared back at my angry face. Because actually that was exactly what you and your friends thought I should be doing. Girls like me, who boys didn't normally like, should be grateful for any interest. We couldn't afford to turn down chances like that. Whereas girls like you didn't have to make that choice.

'If that's how it's got to be, then I'd rather not bother.'

'OK, you're right,' you said with a guilty look as you realised exactly what you'd been implying. 'You shouldn't have to compromise. But there must be someone you like, just even a little bit, Hannah.'

For your sake, I did seriously try to think about it. 'No, there isn't anyone.'

'That's what makes people think you're being too picky.'

I shrugged. 'Whatever. I just don't feel interested in any of the boys I know. I can't help that, can I?'

You skewed round so you were facing me full on and looked at me very seriously. 'Hannah, do you think you might be gay?'

I snorted. 'No, Jenny. I'm very sure I'm not gay.' And I was sure. I found boys in books attractive, guys in movies too. Just none that I knew in real life.

Ever the optimist, you sat up taller. 'Then you just haven't met the right guy yet,' you said brightly, 'or you're just not ready to, and if that's so, then it's totally OK. The right boy will turn up at the right time.' You said it with complete confidence. I didn't really buy into that at the time.

If you were here with me now, sitting over breakfast at Wolfscott, it's what you'd remind me of – that conversation in the tree house. 'See, I was right,' you'd say.

CHAPTER 24

We need to go down to the police station again. Mr Cadwallader arranges a car for us. It's the same driver as before.

'Oliver will take you over and wait for you,' he says to me as I look for Dad in the courtyard where he told me to meet him. 'Your father has gone to collect his phone. He'll be back in a moment. He asked if you could wait for him here.'

'Oh, OK.'

I feel a bit weird getting in the Cadwalladers' big BMW by myself while the driver, Oliver, is left standing by it, waiting for Dad, so I shuffle around on the gravel instead, pretending to look at the stained glass in one of the castle windows.

'Any news about your sister?'

I turn round. Oliver is talking to me. He's about twenty-five with a lean face and hard eyes. He wouldn't be bad looking if his eyes were softer.

'Um, no, not yet.'

'Pretty girl, your sister.'

'Er, yeah.'

'I used to drive her about a bit with the kids if Mr C didn't need the car.' He laughs. 'I'd rather take her out than him though – the view's nicer and she's got a better temper. Although his temper's all right with the girls here, especially the pretty ones like Jenny.'

I nod, not really sure what to say to that.

'You look a lot like her.' His eyes trail down and then up again. He makes no effort to hide it either.

'So people say.' I want to go back into the hotel, away from him, but can't think of an excuse.

'You must be worried about her,' he says and his eyes fix on my breasts. I fold my arms reflexively, wishing I was wearing a baggier top. Do I imagine he smiles slightly as he looks away to the door? 'Your dad must be worried too.'

'Yes, he is,' I snap at him.

Dad comes out and my relief is huge. We get into the car together and Oliver takes us off towards town. But every time I look up, his eyes are watching me through the rear-view mirror and he's wearing that slight smirk. I hate guys like him, who make you feel uncomfortable just for being a girl, like they have the right to leer at you whenever they want.

He's freaking me out so I glare at him through the mirror, but his smirk only widens like he's amused. I'm glad when we get to the station and we can get away from him.

Coombs has no news for us on the search, but we already knew that. 'We've examined the CCTV from the streets around the bank, but we're not getting much. We may have picked up Jenny with a companion, but the film is particularly poor so we'll have to send it away to be enhanced,' he tells us. 'We'll carry on searching through other footage from the area in the hope we see them together again or pick up better footage. On another camera we might be able to do an ID.'

'OK, but what happens now?' Dad asks.

'Given the text Hannah has just had, coupled with the CCTV footage, it's looking more likely that we have a missing persons inquiry. That's the angle I'm going with now. It could be that Jenny is acting of her own free will, but everyone we've spoken to, including yourselves, is clear that this behaviour is totally out of character for her. I think we have to assume that she's either being coerced into something or that she's being held against her will at the moment. Either way, that makes her vulnerable. We won't continue close searching of new areas unless we have some compelling evidence to do so. Right now I think it's better to redirect our efforts into a new appeal for sightings, and to show the bank clip of Jenny to jog the public's memory. Somebody may remember seeing her on that day with a companion. The bank footage is excellent so let's utilise that. Let's appeal again and keep it fresh in the minds of the people on the street. We may have some success with that.'

'When will that happen?'

'I've got the media on board. We'll run some edited highlights of the two of you from the first appeal, along with this new sighting.'

'What if nobody comes forward?' I ask.

Coombs nods. 'Good question. What you need to do, Hannah, is keep in touch with her. Try to encourage her to give more away. I'm going to set up a meeting with our criminal profiler about how to do that. Strictly speaking, her role is more about assisting us to catch criminals, but she's good on missing persons in my experience so I'd like you to talk to her. She wants to come out to you, wants to get a feel for the place as she's never seen Wolfscott and she thinks it might help her link into Jenny's frame of mind.'

'It sounds good. When?'

'She'll come over this afternoon if that's all right.'

'The sooner the better,' Dad replies.

'Great. We're done here then. Heather will be round this afternoon.' Coombs stands up and shakes hands and we make our way out.

The slimy Oliver is waiting to take us back. He does that

creepy thing of watching me again on the way home. I scoot out of the car as soon as I can when it stops, but he gets out too and I can feel his eyes following me as I go inside.

The bird demonstrations are on so there's no point going to look for Harry. I wander through the coffee lounge on the way out to the garden at the back while Dad goes to find Mr Cadwallader. It's busy in there. Tom's serving behind the counter and gives me a friendly wave as I go past.

Outside there's a chair free at an empty table. The sky is overcast and most people have stayed indoors, but I want fresh air. It's good to smell grass and not the stale air of a police station. After about ten minutes, Tom comes out with a pad.

'It's mad in there today,' he exclaims, sitting down in a chair beside me. 'Can I get you anything?'

'Oh, er . . . some kind of coffee?'

'What about a frappe? Coffee in crushed ice? It's humid today. Might make you feel perkier?'

'Yeah, that'll be good. Thanks.'

'Have you had lunch? No? OK, I'll get them to make you a panini too. Back in a minute.'

He takes my order inside and then returns. 'So how did it go this morning?'

'All right. I have to see someone this afternoon to talk about Jenny.'

'Who?'

'A criminal profiler, but she does missing persons work as well. She wants to see if there's anything more I know that could help work out where Jenny is.'

'So they do think she's alive then?'

'Yeah, but there wasn't anything found on the search so they're going to repeat the appeal on TV, this time with some new pictures of her at a bank in town the day before she disappeared. She was with someone.'

'She was with someone? Who?'

'I don't know. You can't see that on the footage.'

'Ah, never mind. Overall it's good news though.' He grins. 'Oops, getting busy again in there. Must get back.' He gives my shoulder a reassuring pat and rushes off.

I'd meant to ask him about creepy Oliver, but I can do it when he serves the food. However, it's a girl who brings my coffee and panini out. 'If Tom's got a second, could you tell him there's something I wanted to ask him?'

She raises her eyebrows at me in a knowing way that's not at all pleasant. I guess girls ask for him a lot. Maybe she's even into him herself. Anyway he doesn't come out, so when I go back inside I look for him, but he's nowhere in sight. I'll have to catch him later.

Heather the profiler shows up soon after lunch. 'Somewhere quiet,' she replies when I ask her where she wants to go. Dad's on the phone to Mom so I suggest my room.

I give her the lowdown on you and then she asks to see the texts.

'Hmm, she does seem like she's ready to open up a bit more. Here's what I think you should do. Keep telling her you miss her and want her back, but don't go overboard with that as she might feel pressurised. If she starts replying to you more often, then hold off on that a bit and try to get her into more of a conversation. Ask her questions about what she's texted you. So now I think you should send her a text with "What did you find out? Are you able to tell me?" and a kiss or however you normally sign off.'

'OK.' I do what she asks.

'Let's keep track of how long she takes between each text to reply. I want to see if a pattern starts to appear – if certain replies make her more or less likely to respond. It seems very random at the moment. Let's see if we can change that.'

I guess that makes sense. She tells me I have to contact her with responses as soon as possible after they come in and she'll give me more guidance on how to reply then.

As I see her out, Oliver is hanging around. It looks like he's doing the valet parking. 'I'll get your car for you, madam,' he says. He gives me another of those slimy sideways glances as he leaves. I feel rude, but I make my excuses and leave Heather to wait on her own.

When I poke my head around the bar, Tom is there, polishing glasses. I grab a stool.

'Hey, there's something I wanted to ask you. You know Oliver, the driver –' And I stop because Tom's face screws up in distaste.

'What about him?'

'Did Jenny know him?'

'Yeah, she didn't like him. None of the girls here do. He pervs at them too much.'

'Oh. I don't like him either.'

Tom puts the glass down and leans across the bar to whisper to me. 'You should stay away from him. He's strange.'

'Yeah, thanks, I will. He said something weird about Mr Cadwallader too – about him treating the girls differently, especially the pretty ones.'

Tom lifts an eyebrow. 'Did he now? He'd better not let Mr C, or Mrs C for that matter, hear him say that. Not that he hasn't got a point.'

'Really?'

'Mrs C keeps her husband on a short leash, put it that way. That's why I was surprised she took to Jenny so much.'

I'm less surprised because everyone takes to you. I give him a smile and go find Dad. He's out back, sitting on a bench with his head in his hands, but he looks up and smiles when he hears me coming.

'Want to go for a walk, honey?'

He looks like he needs company so I defer my plan to visit Harry. We're by the moat when I feel my phone buzz in my pocket. There's a message.

I can't tell you yet, but soon xo

CHAPTER 25

I still want to speak to the guy Harry works with about your disappearance and I've been thinking of how to set that up. The answer comes to me when I'm watching Harry train Merlin in the early morning. I'm beginning to love this part of the day. Everything is as clear as spring water at this time and hope has put on clean, fresh clothes for a new day.

The thing to do is to find a way to engage Steve in conversation and that's what's been puzzling me. As Merlin dives on to the lure, it comes to me. I do just what Jenny did and ask him about the birds. I have an in because of Harry. If I go round and hang out with Harry while he's working, I can just casually start chatting with Steve and then work round to you. The thing is, I've got it in my head now that the most likely person to know something he's not telling is Steve. You used to talk to him, and there's just something about how Harry described that and how he described Steve that makes me suspicious. Now Cassie's not around, he's my best option.

You'll have spotted the flaw, I know. Me and chatting casually – doesn't really go, does it? But I'll try. I may not succeed, but at this moment, with the rays of sun breaking through the mist to promise a good day, it feels possible.

I've briefed Harry on the plan before I turn up at the cages for his and Steve's morning check of the birds.

'I feel a bit weird. Like I'm setting him up or something.'

'Don't you want to do it then?'

'Yes, I said I'd help, but it just feels off.' He shrugs. 'I'll get over it.'

'If the conversation falls off, can you step in and get it going again?'

He looks horrified. Actually, to most people he probably just looks a bit surprised given he has the most shuttered face I've ever seen, but I'm learning to know him better. 'Me? Er, I'll try, but it's not really something I'm good at.'

'I know, but you're OK talking to him – you work with him.'

He frowns. 'Yeah, talking to him about the birds. This is different. No, I'll try. Let's just do it before I think about it too much.'

We walk around to the cages together and Steve is coming

down the path from the other direction. Harry gets there first and unlocks the cages.

'Hi,' says Steve as he comes up to where I'm waiting by the posts for the birds to be brought out. 'Morning, Harry,' he calls into the cages.

There's a muffled reply.

'Come to watch?' Steve asks pleasantly.

'Yes, I was watching Harry fly Merlin this morning and he said it would be OK for me to come and see the others close up. Is that all right?'

'No problem at all,' Steve says, taking a falcon from Harry as he emerges from the cages. 'Here, give him to me. You get another one – ta.' He brings the bird over to one of the smaller posts and starts to tether it. 'You're Jenny's sister, aren't you?'

'Yes, Hannah, hi. Harry says Jenny used to come over and look at the birds too.'

He nods. 'She did. Any news of her? I see the police coming in and out of here a lot.'

'Nothing specific yet.'

'They found nothing on the search? I saw them up there doing that. Worried me that they might have thought it was necessary.' He takes another bird to help Harry. 'I think we're all hoping that she's just taken off somewhere.'

'So are we. No, they found nothing.'

'That's good, I think. So what do they think's happened?'

'There's another appeal today. She was seen in a bank in town with someone the day before she disappeared.' I watch his face carefully as I tell him that.

'Really? Who was it?'

I can't see any sign of recognition, guilt, nothing . . . darn! 'They can't see from the footage yet, which is why they're doing the appeal.'

He sighs. 'I hope she comes back soon. Your dad must be worried sick. I have two daughters – I know how I'd feel if one of them was missing. She's such a nice girl too. My wife's mother is sick and she keeps having to go off to Devon to look after her, so Jenny takes the girls out with the Cadwallader kids sometimes to help me out.'

That sounds more interesting. So his wife's away a lot. And he and Jenny must have been talking some about that for her to know he needed help. 'How did she seem then?'

Harry passes me and tethers an owl close by. He seems to linger over it and I sense he's waiting around in case I need help.

'She was her usual self,' Steve answers. 'This is what I don't understand. I saw her the day before she disappeared too and she didn't seem any different to how she always was.'

'She didn't seem worried, or excited, or more quiet than usual, or –'

'No, absolutely no different to normal. She mentioned going into town, I seem to remember on that last day . . . which is when you said she was seen at the bank.'

He says it like it's just occurred to him – he's very plausible. Is he being straight up here or was she with him and he's trying to cover his tracks?

'It's so weird,' I reply.

He nods. I'm struggling now. This isn't going anywhere useful. I glance at Harry and he picks up like my wingman.

He hands the eagle owl over to Steve. 'Do you know if Jenny was . . . I don't know . . . stressed about anything before she disappeared? She used to chat to you – did she ever mention anything like that?'

'You mean was she upset about something weeks ago? I can't think of anything . . . but you might have a point. Maybe this was something she'd planned well in advance. '

I don't say to either of them that what they're describing doesn't sound too much like you. Then again, I question what I know about you every day now.

'You know what, Harry, I do remember her being really fed up at one point. It was easily a month before she went.'

My ears prick up. 'What was wrong with her?'

'She didn't say. I think she'd had some kind of argument with her mother and she was upset about that, but I don't know what it was about. She was just a bit . . . mopey.'

OK, that's news to me. That's something I need to speak to Mom about.

A little voice near my elbow makes me jump. 'Daddy, you forgot your sandwiches!'

A little girl with Steve's eyes is standing by me, holding a lunchbox.

'Oh, thanks, love.' He bends down and gives her a kiss. 'This is my eldest, Sammi.'

She looks up at me. 'You look like Jenny.'

'I'm her sister.'

'When's Jenny coming back? We miss her. She used to come round and play with us when Mummy was away. We want her to come for tea again.'

Again? 'For tea with you and your mummy?'

Out of the corner of my eye, I see Steve shift uncomfortably.

'No,' Sammi replies in that way small children do when they think you've said something very silly, 'she didn't come when Mummy was there. Mummy isn't supposed to know – it's our secret.'

'Thank you for bringing my lunch, love. You run back home now,' Steve says, giving her a cuddle and hurrying her back over the grass towards the gate.

Harry and I exchange a look.

Steve's laughing when he comes back, laughing a little bit too much for it to be real. 'Kids are so funny. She begged Jenny to come round for tea once when my wife was away. We said it had to be a secret from her mum because she'd be upset if she knew how much Sammi was missing her. She felt guilty enough about leaving the girls.'

I smile and nod like I believe him. A few moments later he makes an excuse about needing to check supplies and slips off. I think it's to get away from me.

'What did you think of that?' I ask Harry.

He looks glum. 'He could be telling the truth, but it seems shaky. Maybe there was something going on between them. Or maybe there was nothing going on, but he won't tell his wife in case she gets jealous.'

'If he was seeing Jenny, he must know where she is though.'

'Not necessarily. If they argued, she might have gone off because she was upset with him.'

'Oh yeah, good point.' I hesitate. I so want to tell him about the texts, but Coombs said not to tell anyone. Absolutely nobody. It feels wrong, but I should do as he's told me. Also, Dad would go crazy with me if I did. He made me promise not to. Maybe it was Harry he had in mind when he did that. He must have noticed us hanging out together by now, but that's Dad – never asks questions about things like that. He leaves that to Mom.

'I'll keep an eye on him,' Harry says. 'See if he's acting strangely or anything.'

'You mean he could be meeting her?'

'Maybe, but I think it's more likely she'd had a fight with

him and went off. But we could be leaping to massive conclusions here.'

Steve's walking back towards the cages with a bottle in his hand. Harry looks at me.

'I'll see if I can get away for a break in about half an hour. Better if you disappear until then. Let me talk to him a bit more. Maybe I can work out if he's trying to cover up anything.'

It makes sense. I give Harry a quick kiss and then hurry off back into the hotel, making sure to give Steve a cheery wave as I do.

I double-check my phone in case I've missed a reply from you. My text back to you last night asked you to keep talking to me until you could tell me whatever it was you needed to. I hope I've been so preoccupied with Steve that I didn't notice your reply come, but it turns out to be a vain hope – there's still nothing from you.

CHAPTER 26

You still haven't texted me back by the following day and Heather says what I put in my text to you was fine. It was good you replied so quickly. There's nothing more I can do to move things on for now. The cops are doing their thing with the CCTV. They're carrying out door-to-door questioning about Cassie too and maybe that will provide more information. Until then I may as well just hang out with Harry and take my mind off waiting.

So that's pretty much what I do for the next couple of days. We go back to the mere and chill there as the weather's good. I think about questioning Mom on what you guys fought about, but I'd have to tell her how I know and I don't want to explain about Steve. There's probably nothing in it, Harry convinces me, but Mom wouldn't see it that way. I know she'd make a big deal of it and stress.

Harry shows me around a few more places in the area and we spend lots of time training Merlin. Harry says he's really starting to come on. He gets me a gauntlet and we practise flying Merlin between us, which is an important skill for him if he's going to do demonstrations. It's kind of nice for me too because it makes me feel like I'm useful. Merlin's pretty cool. Harry says he likes me. I'll have to take his word for that because I sure can't tell. He stares at me with expressionless yellow eyes. I like him though. Working him is fun.

Harry has a demonstration the next afternoon and it's turned really cold outside so I go and sit in the coffee lounge with a magazine I borrow from one of the tables in reception. I've been there a while when Tom passes and sees me.

'Hi, I'm on my break,' he says, taking the chair next to me. 'So how's Hannah?'

'OK, actually. The police got some calls following the last TV appeal and they're working on those. We're hoping for some good news.'

'That'd be great. I hope so too. So what've you been up to?'

'Just hanging out.'

He laughs. 'Yeah, I saw you yesterday with a new friend.'

'Harry? Yes.' What am I supposed to say? We're seeing each other? He's my boyfriend? Um, I'm not sure how to describe it. It's not like we've talked about it.

'Did he tell you he's my brother?'

My jaw drops and I'm left gaping at him. Harry's his *brother*? Why didn't he say something? 'Um, no!'

'He wouldn't. We're not close. In fact we don't get on much at all.'

I guess they are very different. I'm still trying to process what he's just told me. It's struck me a real blow and I'm kind of reeling.

'I'm your basic friendly type and he's more your antisocial, only-hang-out-with-feathered-friends type.' He grins at me. 'Which is good from your point of view as he's definitely not the cheating kind. Seriously, can you get him to speak though?'

I recover enough to react to that. 'Yeah, I can actually.'

He laughs again. 'Don't get cross. I'm only teasing. Anyway, what I came over to say was that you have taken on board what I said about Oliver, haven't you?'

'Yeah, believe me I'll stay well away from him. He creeps me out.'

'I warned Jenny about him too. He went through this phase when she first came of following her about everywhere. Like, wherever she went, he would suddenly pop up. She avoided him for a while and it stopped, but he can be odd like that. The police checked him out, of course. They checked everyone out. It was like the Spanish Inquisition round here for a few days.

Aubrey was going nuts about how they were all over him.'

'Who's Aubrey?'

'One of the chefs. He's worked here a couple of years, but he's got a criminal record so the police made a beeline for him.'

'What's he like?'

'Aubrey? Kind of a rough guy, but OK. Not creepy like Oliver. He has a girlfriend and she wasn't too happy about the suggestions there could have been something going on between him and Jenny, which is the angle the police were taking. I mean, she works here too so she's seen Jenny and, well, Jenny is a lot prettier than her. I suppose she felt insecure. But at the end of it all, Aubrey had an alibi here on site on the afternoon Jenny disappeared so they left him alone after that.'

OK, so it wasn't Aubrey. What's playing on my mind now I've had time to process it is the revelation that Tom and Harry are brothers.

'You don't look much alike,' I blurt out.

He looks perplexed for a moment. 'Oh, me and Harry? Same dad and different mothers. He's my half-brother.'

That probably explains the not getting on too well part then. 'Ah, I see.' Something I should talk to Harry about rather than Tom, I think. He didn't tell me himself so maybe he doesn't want me to know for some reason. Still, I don't feel good about that – like I've learned something that changes who I thought he was.

'Oops, gotta go. Don't want Mr C breathing down my neck,' Tom says, getting up quickly. 'See you later.'

He rushes off, leaving me still confused, emotions I don't understand churning me up inside. *Harry* . . . that has completely blindsided me . . .

It's no big deal. Lots of brothers don't get on. But I guess it shows me how much I don't know about Harry. But am I supposed to know more about him yet? Boyfriend stuff is so confusing.

And again I'm wishing you were here so I could ask you things like this.

I guess I have to suck it up and learn to deal on my own. Any day now, you could come back and Dad and I will leave. Which makes Harry and I as an item the dumbest idea ever. But that doesn't change how I feel about him. What I'm not entirely sure about is how he feels about me. Harry and I are going to need to talk, which Harry hates doing. But what's the alternative?

I check my phone again, like a reflex. Nothing.

But then just as I go to put it away, the text message icon flashes up.

It won't be much longer. Promise. This is big and I need time to get my head around it.

Whoa, Jenny, what did you get yourself into? I text you back:

OK, but keep talking to me. I get scared when I don't hear from you.

Would Heather say that's too much pressure? This is so tough, Jenny, and I'm trying my best here. I just don't know how to do this right.

CHAPTER 27

'Harry, have you got any time today when we could talk about some stuff?'

We're walking back from flying Merlin in his morning training session.

'What kind of stuff?'

I watch him carefully. 'I was talking to Tom yesterday.'

He flinches and then looks away over to the trees. 'Oh yeah?'

'I didn't know he was your brother. I didn't even know you had a brother.'

'Yeah, well, I'd prefer not to have one.'

'Hmm, he said you guys didn't get on too well.'

'Oh, did he!' Harry finally looks at me again. 'What else did he say?'

'Not much. I was just a bit surprised when he told me, that's all.'

Harry's lip curls. I've never seen him look so hostile before. I had wanted to push this with him, but I'm not sure that's such a good idea. It seems like more than they just don't get along, like maybe they really hate each other.

'Yes, to your original question,' he says in something more like his normal voice and I'm relieved he's himself so quickly again. 'I've got some time now. You can come over to my place if you want and I'll make you breakfast.'

'Sure.' He lives in a cottage in the grounds. He pointed it out to me once, but I've never been inside.

We settle Merlin back in his cage and then we go to the cottage. I don't know if you'll have seen it, Jenny, but it's the tiniest house I've ever come across. Like a little Hansel-and-Gretel-in-the-woods creation.

There's one big main room with a kitchenette in the corner and a wood-burning stove at the other end where there are a couple of comfy chairs. In the middle is a wooden kitchen table. The bedroom door is open and I can see that he's made his bed, which is impressive given the hour he gets up at. And there's nothing lying around on the floor. It's all very neat. Mom would love him.

'Bacon butties OK for breakfast?'

'Bacon what?'

He laughs. 'You'll see. Sit down.'

I take a seat at the table and he busies himself getting bacon and bread out. He flicks the kettle on for coffee while I look around the cottage. The windows are tiny which makes it dark inside. There's little I can see that isn't of practical use, but everything is clean and tidy, just as the other rooms were.

'How is it you have this place then?'

'I didn't have anywhere else to go,' he answers, holding up an egg questioningly. I nod and he cracks it into a skillet. 'My father used to work here. He was the vicar for the estate chapel.'

'Estate?'

'Yeah, the Cadwalladers don't just own the castle, but all the land around here too. Most of it's rented out to tenant farmers and the Cadwallader family have always funded the chapel and the vicar to serve the estate.'

'So where's your dad now?'

'He died a couple of years ago in a fire. The rectory was burned to the ground.'

'Oh, I'm sorry, that's horrible!'

He goes on with his explanation as if he's just told me he has a mild stomach ache, not a dead father, but I'm guessing that's how he deals with heavy stuff. 'Legally, my brother's my guardian until I'm eighteen, but like he told you, we don't get on. At first I stayed with Steve's family in their spare room, but by the time I was sixteen this cottage had become vacant so the Cadwalladers let me live here.'

'What about Tom? Where does he live?'

He gives me a strange look. 'He's got a place in the staff quarters up at the castle, round the back in the mews.' He makes the coffee, keeping an eye on the eggs and bacon. 'The Cadwalladers got on with Dad so they looked out for us when he died. They can be good like that.'

'What about your mom?' I have half an idea already what his answer will be since he's never mentioned her.

'She died when I was nine. Cancer.'

What do you say when your boyfriend tells you he's an orphan? He's stiff-backed in a way that warns me not to make a fuss about it. He's assembling a sandwich and concentrating on that. He squirts some brown sauce on it.

'What's that?' I ask, glad of the distraction.

'HP,' he replies, head turning over his shoulder to give me a grin. 'Trust me, it works.'

He puts a plate of egg and bacon sandwiches in front of me with a mug of coffee, and then sits opposite with the same.

'Bacon butties,' he says, pointing at the sandwich.

'Butties,' I repeat after him, picking one up and taking a bite. I chew and pause. 'OMG, that is awesome.'

He winks at me. It gives his face a cheeky look I haven't seen before and it's wildly cute. 'Told you.'

I debate where we are with our conversation as we eat. He's not going to reopen it, I can see that. As far as he's concerned, he's answered some questions he had to answer and got it over with, so it's at an end. It shouldn't be a surprise – I know this is how he is. Dealing with the theory and the practice is a little different though and I do find myself wanting to probe. To ask what and why and how, and extract more information.

However, his face as he chews the sandwich is perfectly content now because I've stopped interrogating him. Every instinct I have wants to wheedle more out of him. I have to lock that down inside me, but I feel it like an itch I can't scratch. I really do want to talk to him about the whole boyfriend/girlfriend thing though. But getting started on that is really difficult.

I wish he'd ask, 'Is there anything else you wanted to talk about?' That would make it so easy, but – and I laugh at myself – that's never going to happen.

He looks up. 'What're you laughing about?' he says, smiling.

OK, it's an in. Maybe not a very promising one, but it's the only one I have. 'When Tom mentioned you yesterday, I wasn't sure how to answer. I was just laughing at how the heck I was supposed to bring that up with you. But I guess I just did!'

He bristles as soon as I mention his brother's name so I wait to let the rest of what I said sink in. After a moment, he replies. 'What do you mean?'

That's a start. At least he's asked me and not just dropped it like I thought he might. I take a thoughtful sip of coffee to prepare myself. 'It's kind of awkward. Like he was making out we were seeing each other and then I got to thinking, if we are actually assumed to be seeing each other, does that makes us, like . . .'

I have to stop. He looks appalled and I'm scared to go on. Plus, the words boyfriend and girlfriend are sticking in my throat. I just cannot get them out.

'What do you think?' I ask in desperation.

'Haven't thought about it.' His voice is as close to a squeak as a boy can get.

This is awful. I want to die. He's just staring at me like he's hoping I'll disappear.

'OK, let's forget about it.' I get up hurriedly. 'I should get back anyway.'

He stands too. 'No! Um, I mean, it's obviously bothering you so . . . I just hadn't thought about it . . . so I, er, need to . . . Just sit down for a minute!'

It comes out more like a command than a request, but I'm not going to take offence. I'm finding this as difficult as he is. I sit back down and fiddle with my nails.

'It's sort of difficult,' he mumbles. 'You'll be going home eventually. If you weren't, I'd want to keep seeing you.' When I risk a glance up, he's fixed his eyes on the table and is scratching at the grain in the wood. I wait a little longer, but he's dried up.

He looks up at me and his eyes plead for help. He can't find the words.

I take in a deep breath. 'So do you think we're, um, seeing each other now?'

'Yes,' he says in a rush.

There's a pause and we search each other's faces, equally confused.

'Do you?' he asks, his eyes flickering around nervously.

'Yes. I just wanted to check you did too.'

He heaves a huge sigh. I guess it's of relief. 'Cool.'

He gets up and comes to kneel in front of me. He's tall enough that if he tugs my head down a little he can kiss me easily.

Wrapped in his arms, nothing seems difficult any more. This is so much easier than speaking. I can tell from the way he kisses me that he finds that too. It's as if he's trying to put everything into this kiss that he can't put into words. And that's OK, it really is. I just need to learn his language.

We're on borrowed time, we both know that. I didn't go looking for this thing that's between me and him. It jumped out on me and caught me up before I had time to know what was happening. And it's done now – I'm in deep and there's no way to escape. It's like drowning – I'm falling further and further down into this ocean that appears to have no bottom and it's scary but painless at the same time.

From the outside, it must look like the wrongest thing for me to fall in love with him now, but I'm the one falling and from in here it feels as if it's the rightest thing ever.

He pulls away and looks into my eyes. Gentle fingers stroke my cheek like feathers brushing my skin.

'I want to be with you,' he whispers. 'I don't know how to say anything else.'

And it is more than enough.

I never knew it could be like this for me, Jenny. It's nothing like you've ever described with Trey – it is so much more. He's everything I ever thought could never really exist. When I'm with him, I'm more me than I've ever been with anyone, even you. Every cell in my body feels tuned to his frequency.

CHAPTER 28

Another day goes by before I hear from you and, when I do, I'm relaxing with Harry while he's on his lunch break.

I'm trying to find out what Mom wouldn't tell me.

It takes me a second to process that and then I know I need to show Dad this text straight away.

Harry is lying on his back in the grass, watching the clouds drift lazily across the sky. 'What's up?' he asks, seeing me looking at my phone. It's on the tip of my tongue to tell him, but I can't.

'Dad just texted me. I need to go see him right now.'

I'm pleased he looks disappointed. 'Oh, OK. Will you be around later?'

'After dinner? Yeah, I'll come over to yours for a while.'

He jumps to his feet to walk me back. It's such a very cool

thing, being walked back from somewhere by a boy. It makes me feel special because there's absolutely no need for it. We're within sight of the castle. It's just so we can be together for as long as possible.

Dad is bewildered by the text. 'I thought you would know what she's talking about,' I tell him.

'I have no idea. I'll ask your mom obviously, but I'm as confused as you are.'

He goes to call her and I'm left to sit and wait again.

But he looks just as confused when he comes back. 'Your mom says Jenny asked her for some information about tracing her family tree and Mom wouldn't tell her. She swears that's all Jenny has asked her for. But I don't understand this, honey. Jenny isn't going to go running off and pretend to disappear just to trace her family tree.'

'Why wouldn't Mom tell her?'

He rubs his forehead. 'Your mom doesn't like talking about her past. She finds it really painful and we have to respect that. I'm surprised at Jenny reacting like this. She's always been so understanding and patient before.'

Hmm, but you and I had talked about Mom and her refusal to tell us anything. I figured it was a bit melodramatic that we couldn't know even one single little thing. You just found it annoying because you wanted that connection, that missing part of your identity.

Dad and I sit tossing ideas between us until Coombs and Heather show up. Coombs is alert and ready for action as soon as he reads the text. Heather leans back in her chair and looks long and hard at my phone.

'What did your wife say?'

Dad tells her the gist of it.

'She talk to you about it?'

'No.'

Coombs nods slowly. 'You know we're going to have to look into this.'

'My wife says she has no family left here. She was an only child.'

'It sounds like Jenny didn't believe that. She could be looking for extended family – distant cousins, that type of thing.'

Dad stands up and paces around. 'I cannot see why that would make her run off this way. Firstly, it's totally not Jenny to do that and secondly I can't see how it would help.'

'Could she be trying to make her mother feel bad in order to obtain the information she wants?'

'I can see how that could be plausible with anyone but Jenny, but this *is* Jenny we're talking about and I just don't buy that.'

'No, I don't either,' says Heather suddenly. 'We're missing something here. I don't know what, but . . . there's something niggling away at me about this.'

I know what she means. These assumptions we're

all making have started to bug me too.

'What do I reply to her?'

'Ask her what she means,' Coombs says.

I look at Heather. She shrugs. 'Try it. I doubt somehow you'll get an answer. If she wanted to tell you, she could have done that from the outset, but I can't see that it will do any harm.'

'All right.' I send the text while they're all watching.

'I'm going to start by checking any computer here she had access to again,' Coombs says. 'If she's looking for family information, she'll be using certain sites. As we weren't looking for anything of that nature, it could have been overlooked in our initial searches. Let's see if she's been digging around for information about that. I'll check with the local library too in case she went there, although it's a long shot. It's hardly open now since the cutbacks, but we need to follow it up. We have some news on her bank account in the US too. She was depositing some of her wages in there but not all. It looks like she was taking some and putting it into the account she had in Cassie's name, but for what reason? It does look as if she may have been planning something.'

I'm angry with you again now, and I'm angry with Mom too for not opening up to Dad. This is not a game and I want to yell that at the both of you. Look at all of us here trying to get our heads around whatever this is you're trying to pull, Jenny. Why can't you just tell us?

CHAPTER 29

I keep turning Heather's words over and over in my brain for the next twenty-four hours. You and the family tree . . . it was Tom who brought it up. I'll speak to him about it. Luckily he's in the bar that afternoon.

'Hi,' he says, rushing past. 'Be with you when I can.' There's a long-legged girl in the seat across from me who tries to catch his eye and smile – one of the hotel guests staying with her parents, I think. From her smirk of satisfaction when he's gone, she succeeded. She eyes me like I'm something she just found under a stone.

By the time Tom comes back, I'm bored of counting the leaves on the fake fig tree by my seat and I see the girl scowl as he sits down beside me.

'Haven't got long. Mr C is in a foul mood today. What's up?'

'I wanted to speak to you about Jenny and what she told you about trying to trace her family tree, but if it's a bad time –'

He glances around. 'It's not great right now. But look, the person you really need to speak to about all of that is one of the other waiters – Michael. He helped her with it. I only heard it second hand. Come back after dinner. He gets off shift about half nine. I'll arrange for you to meet him in the bar.'

Harry and I hang together after he finishes work. It's a cool evening and he's got the log burner in his cottage on a gentle heat. I curl up on his knee in the battered armchair in front of the fire and he plays with my hair.

I'm more content in silence with him than I could ever imagine being with another boy, however easily he might talk. There's more to life than pointless chatter.

People say silence is lonely. It's not lonely with Harry. It's peaceful, restful, calm and safe. I don't need to say all this to him because he has no use for talk like that. He understands when I lay my head on his shoulder and am happy.

Our time together goes all too soon and he walks me back up to the castle to meet Dad for dinner. Dad is still brooding over yesterday's text from you. He leaves me afterwards to talk to Mom and I tell him that's fine – I'm going to go read or something.

Tom's serving in the bar as he said he would be. He waves me over to a seat in the corner. There's a guy sitting there who's wearing round, geeky-cool kind of glasses, with floppy hair and the sort of forgettable face that makes you feel comfortable and like him. He's about Tom's age and I think I've seen him in the restaurant before.

'Hi, I'm Michael.' He smiles at me in a friendly way.

'Hannah, hi and thanks for agreeing to talk to me.'

'No problem. Anything to help find Jenny. So what do you want to know?'

'Tom said you were helping Jenny trace her family tree. Can you tell me about that?'

'Yeah, sure. We were talking one day after work and I was telling her that I'd been working on my own family tree. She was interested and I explained how I went about it. I think by that time I'd got five generations back. She was fascinated by the idea of being able to do something similar with your family in the US, but she said it made her sad she couldn't do the same for her English family. We spoke about it a few times and I showed her the resources I'd collected and the sites I used.'

'Do you know if she started to do any research herself?'

'She said she was going to have a go. Then a few days later she said she'd spoken to her mother who really didn't want her to.'

'Was she OK with that?'

'No, she was fed up. She'd already thought she'd got some leads. She managed to find out some basic information about her grandparents. Things I think she already knew, but she was happy to see she was on the right road.'

'So she got mad at what Mom said?'

'Not mad. Disappointed is more how I'd describe it. But then a bit later, when I asked her how she was getting on, she told me she'd changed her mind. She said bringing it up with your mother was selfish of her because it made your mum so unhappy and she hated doing that so she was dropping it.'

'She was dropping it?' This really didn't make sense.

Michael nods. 'Yes, that's what she said.'

Well, he couldn't be clearer than that. Jenny, what are you up to?

I thank Michael, wave goodnight to Tom and make my way to bed. But it's a long time before I sleep.

CHAPTER 30

What I decide in the end is that it comes down to this: the gatekeeper of the information I need is Mom and I have to talk to her. I make an excuse to Dad and to Harry about a headache and needing to sleep, but then I call home from the hotel phone by my bed. I just hope this gives me my answers.

I lie on the bed with the phone cradled between the pillow and my ear. 'Mom, hi, I need to talk to you.'

'Are you OK, honey?'

'Yeah, I'm fine. Has Dad told you about the latest texts?' I know he has, but I want to hear her reaction for myself.

Her voice flattens to close me down straight away. 'Yes, he's told me. I don't understand what she means.'

'Well, what did you say to her, Mom?'

'I've already explained this to your father.'

I sit up. 'Fine, but it's not Dad or you she's texting. And that puts me under a lot of pressure so I think I deserve to hear an explanation too.'

'There's no need to raise your voice, Hannah. If it were up to me, you wouldn't even be there. You'd be at home.'

'I want Jenny found!'

'We all want that.'

'Start acting like it then! You know something and you're not telling me. And Jenny was mad at you because you wouldn't tell her something either. If we're going to find her, we need to know.'

'There's no possible way that anything Jenny was asking me can have any bearing on where she is now. It's ridiculous.'

'So tell me what you fought about.'

There's a long sigh. 'We didn't fight, Hannah. We had a discussion about something and we had a difference of opinion, but it really wasn't a fight.'

'So what happened then? Mom, I need to know.' I lie back on the pillow.

'It was months ago. Jenny wanted information about my family so she could trace her family tree. I refused.'

'But why?'

'Because it's my business, Hannah, and I don't want to get into what was a very unhappy time again.'

'Well, obviously it was a bigger deal to Jenny than that.'

'But this is the thing, honey. It wasn't. She was mad at first, then we spoke and she said it was fine and she understood.'

'Mom, think carefully. Maybe we got this wrong. Is there anything else she could have asked you that you might have said no to? Anything else that she could possibly have meant in that text?'

'Honey, I have racked my brains over and over. I have absolutely no idea what she's talking about. None at all. If I do work it out, I promise you that I'll call you and Dad straight away.'

I tell her I love her and ask about Brandon, then ring off, but I am more confused now that ever. What are you up to, Jenny? Are you trying to get a response from Mom? Is that what the text was about? But it doesn't make sense why you would do that when you could just speak to her. We don't have that kind of weird relationship with Mom where you'd need to resort to crazy plotting like that.

I hope Mom figures out what you're talking about because, if she doesn't, the rest of us don't stand a chance.

CHAPTER 31

Being with Harry gives me stolen moments of sanity in what is more and more a world that's turning to chaos. My sister's missing, now her friend's missing and it feels like we're getting nowhere in finding them. But with Harry it's like a time warp – I step away into a suspended place, far away from reality, and we hide there until we have to come out. There, everything makes sense.

I learn that a brush of his fingers down my neck can make my skin sing. I learn that there are no eyes in the world where I find more peace than his. I learn that when this is over it will feel like my world is ending and I cannot bear to think of that so I push it away to the outer reaches of my mind.

We are sitting outside his cottage in the afternoon sunlight, leaning against a tree and watching dragonflies dance over the long grass.

'How did you get into working with birds?' I ask, twining my fingers around his.

'It was when we moved here. I used to go and watch Steve right from when we first came. Steve sort of took me under his wing.' He grins. 'No pun intended, and he showed me how to fly them, how to look after them. When I was old enough, he gave me an after-school job helping him out.'

I imagine a junior Harry with large, serious dark eyes. It's a cute picture.

'What about you? What do you want to do when you finish school?'

It's rare for him to ask me something out of the blue that way.

'I really don't know yet.'

He nods sympathetically. And then smiles as he looks at our hands together. He raises my fingers to his mouth and places a feather kiss on the tips.

I am beyond regretting falling in love with him by now. Bad idea or not, it's how it is and there's no helping it. I wonder if we'll ever put how we feel into words and if we don't if that is even a problem. There are moments when I think I need to hear it back from him and then other times, like now, when he has my palm curled against his cheek and he looks as if there's nowhere he would rather be than here with me, that I think I need to grow up and stop being needy. He is what he is and I love him for that. I can't want to change him when it suits me to satisfy some stupid need.

'What's it like here in winter? I guess it's beautiful.'

He chuckles and I feel the vibration of his laughter in my hand. 'It's mostly muddy. No, it is beautiful, especially in the morning when the frost is lying over everything and the ground is hard. We don't get much snow, but when we do it's the most beautiful place you've ever seen. Don't you love how the snow muffles sound? It's quieter on snowy days. You can't hear the traffic around here then because the lanes are usually blocked for hours in the morning until the tractors dig them out. Taking the birds out then is one of the best feelings in the world.'

'What are the other best feelings?'

His gaze doesn't flicker. He's watching the dragonflies in the distance. 'Here, now,' he answers, half in a whisper.

I tuck my head under his chin, snuggling in closer, and in return he holds me tighter. I can feel the strong muscle of his arms around me, a circle of security, of comfort. But one which makes my blood fizz hot too.

I tilt my chin so that my lips can meet his. This is no slow, languorous kiss. This is a kiss that tells him he makes my world cartwheel when I see him, makes me burn when we're together. His lips give me that same heat back. I turn in his arms to deepen the kiss.

When we stop, we're both out of breath and flushed. His eyes, his fingertips brushing my cheek, both ask the same question.

'Yes,' I say.

He kisses me hard again and his hands slide under my T-shirt, caressing bare skin that seems to spark under his touch. I slide my hands up his bare back, over his chest, feeling smooth skin taut over hard, lean muscle.

I'm shaking all over. This is addictive, a narcotic in the blood. But if I don't hold back I'll be destroyed when I have to leave here. I'll stay as long as I dare though, nerves so alive to every feeling. Exploring him and learning the map of his body as he explores mine.

In the end, we stop together. We both know the danger in carrying on and we both know we're living out of time and space here. If we hadn't been, I don't know if we could have found the strength to pull away.

CHAPTER 32

There's so much you don't know. I can't tell you like this. You'll have to wait. I can't say any more now.

I curse when I read your message, then I text you back immediately.

When will you be able to?

To my astonishment, you text me back straight away.

When I know I can trust you.

You can always trust me.

There's a long pause, and then,

You must do as I ask then. It's very important. Tell no one.

And there's the sticking point. I should call Heather straight away about this, or speak to Dad. More than ever I want to tell Harry what's going on, but if I do, you can't trust me.

I have to hold on to the Jenny I know and I have to believe in you. I guess that means doing what you ask even though this feels so wrong. So I won't tell anyone. For you.

OK, I promise.

It's very important.

I promise.

Thank you. I have to go now, but I'll be in touch again as soon as I can. It may take a few days.

I love you xoxox

But there's no reply.

That's the closest thing we've had to a conversation in weeks and my heart fills with pain, missing you all over again. But you seem changed, different. I suppose that's inevitable and I just have to be there for you when you do come back.

Please let that be soon.

I go downstairs to find Dad. He's in the bar, reading a newspaper. Tom is working and he comes over and takes my order – a Diet Coke.

'I think we're getting to about our limit here, Hannah.' Dad puts the paper down to see how I'll react.

'What do you mean?'

'I don't think we're getting any closer to finding Jenny and I think your mom is right. You should go home.'

Tom brings my drink over.

'I can't go home now. What if she tries to contact me again?'

If only I could tell him . . .

'No, Hannah. Heather said she thinks it's all stalling for time. I don't know what Jenny's game is, but I'm not having this affect you any longer. You should go back home. School starts soon and you need to get ready for that. Whatever's going on with Jenny, I will deal with it.'

'Dad, not now. A few more days. Let's just try a few more days and then we can talk about it. Please.'

Because I really do believe you'll be back by then.

'I can't see the point, Hannah, I really can't.'

'What if she's not stalling? What if she's getting ready to come back?'

He shakes his head. 'What if she's got herself into some really bad trouble? I don't want you getting caught up in all that. You've been through enough. It's time to put a stop to it. I'm going to book you a flight back home.'

'Dad, please, just a few more days. Please. I promise I won't argue after that. Just give it until the end of the week.'

He glares at me and, for what it's worth, I glare back at him because he needs to know I'm not backing down. I just promised you that you could trust me.

Me. Not Dad or Mom. It's me you're going to get in contact with to come back to us, I just know it. If I leave now, what will you do? So I have to fight to stay whether Dad likes it or not. I have to do whatever it takes to win, even if it means fighting dirty.

'You know, if Mom had listened to Jenny, then she might have understood her better and we might know what's going on in Jenny's head right now. You're making the same mistake. You and Mom need to listen to us. We may be kids but we're not dumb, Dad.'

It hurts him like a blow to the chest. I see that and I feel guilty, but I must do this for you.

'It's only a few days, Dad. How can it hurt?'

He gets up. 'I need to call your mom then and tell her. She was looking forward to having you home as soon as we could get you a flight.'

I grab his hand. 'Thanks, Dad.'

He nods sadly and walks out of the bar like the whole world is on his shoulders. I know how badly this is getting to him and I've just made it a whole lot worse.

There's a tap on my shoulder. It's Tom. 'You OK?'

I try to smile and nod, but I don't pull it off very well.

'If you were older, I'd say you needed a stiff whisky,' he says, smiling back. 'I can probably get a hot chocolate made for you though. You know, I had a girlfriend who used to say chocolate was essential food for girls.'

'That'd be good, thanks.' I slump back in the chair, feeling suddenly worn out. I don't know how much more of this any of us can take.

CHAPTER 33

It's strange what you remember in the early hours of the morning when sleep won't come. I wake well before dawn, far too early to get up and with no inclination to do so. What I really want is to go back to sleep, but that lovely fog has cleared too far for me to imagine there's any chance of that happening. Instead I lie there awake and my brain keeps thinking.

If you're back soon, then it won't be long before we leave for home. If you're not back, then Dad's sending me home in a few days anyway. Either way, what it amounts to is that it's nearly the end for me and Harry.

And I remember how one day I came home to find you upstairs on your bed in a flood of tears.

'Shut the door, Hannah, I don't want Mom and Dad hearing.'

I could hardly make out what you were saying, you were crying so hard. You buried your face in the pillows. I hardly recognised you. You'd been crying for a long time before I came in and your face was swollen, your eyes red and puffy. You looked like hell actually.

I closed the door behind me.

You turned your head slightly again. 'No, I meant you go away too.'

I ignored you and sat down on the edge of your bed and waited. And waited.

In the end, I wondered how someone could go on crying for so long. There was no point asking you why you were crying so much because you were in such a state that I'd have found it hard to make out your answer. Besides, I had an idea what it might be.

That morning, when you went out, you hadn't been your usual cheerful, talkative self. I watched you at breakfast. Were you ever so slightly paler? You were definitely preoccupied with something. I tried to make conversation to see if you'd tell me, but I don't think you even noticed, answering me with a set of distracted grunts and staring into space like you weren't even there with us.

I should have put an arm round you or stroked your back, I guess. Something comforting. But tears make me so uncomfortable and I didn't know how to deal with you when you were so far gone so instead I sat there and waited for you to stop. Because you had to stop eventually, right?

And eventually you did. You turned round and said, 'Why are you here? Because you're sure not helping.'

You reminded me of me then. That rarely happened. But you were mad at me for sitting there and not trying to comfort you when, truth was, I had no idea where to start.

'What's wrong?'

'Everything,' you said and buried your head again. It was so melodramatic it could have been funny except it wasn't because this wasn't you, all this hysteria. I was a little bit scared of you in this state. You were so far from how you normally behaved that I didn't know how to reach you.

I moved up the bed so I was sitting beside your head. After a while, your fingers reached out and held mine. I think that reassured both of us, though the idea, of course, was that it was meant to comfort you, but like I said, I was getting scared by then.

Finally, you rolled on to your side. The tears had slowed enough to have kind of stopped, at least for a while.

'What happened?'

You shook your head at me and I passed you a tissue from beside the bed because nobody cries that much and stays pretty. There was snot everywhere and you needed to clean up.

After that, you looked a bit better, which was a relief.

'Trey called me last night. He said we needed to talk today.'

'Oh.'

'Trey never says we need to talk, not like that, not all serious, so I knew something was wrong.'

'So what is it?'

'He wants to break up.'

OK, so I expected you to be pretty messed up by that. You and Trey had been together a while; I forget exactly how long. But you were one of those couples that everyone in school always thought of as a couple. People never spoke of you singly any more.

'Why?'

'He says it won't work because he's at college and I'm still here in school. He said our worlds were too different and too far away.'

It had been a bone of contention for a while that you wanted to go visit him one weekend and he kept on putting you off, saying he had a football game, or he had to study, always some excuse.

'I think he might have a new girlfriend, Hannah.'

That was probably it.

'He said guys at college with girls who visit all the time get laughed at, especially if they're high-school girls. He said they don't get treated nicely by the other college kids and I

181

wouldn't like that. I'd get upset, he said, and he wouldn't be able to do anything about it so that'd upset him too.' You sat up, your face suddenly angry as you processed everything. 'He said he was doing it for me, Hannah. For ME!'

You hurled the tissue. But tissues don't go very far when you throw them and it fluttered sadly to the bed. What you really wanted was a rock to hurl. Preferably at his head, in my opinion.

'He's not worth it, Jenny. He's not worth getting this hurt over.'

You stared at me as if I was stupid, and I know now that I was. 'You don't get to choose, Hannah. I don't want to feel like this. I love him and I thought he loved me. I guess I was wrong. That hurts more than you can imagine. I can't make all that just go away.'

What did I know of love? I didn't know how to help you. To me, Trey wasn't some godlike football player the way a lot of girls in high school saw him. He was a dick who had sometimes made you unhappy by not understanding you, and by putting himself first too much and you not enough. And now he had broken your heart, you were telling me how you felt about it.

I didn't know how to fix a broken heart for you.

'I need a hug,' you said, your face crumpling again.

So I hugged you, and hugged you, and we sat there together. And if willpower could have fixed your heart, it would have been mended right there and then.

I didn't understand then how you felt. I think I'm beginning to now. In the furthest corners of my mind, I can feel the fear growing from a tiny kernel into something that could engulf me if I don't keep holding it at bay by blocking it out as something that won't happen yet . . . not yet . . . still time.

I am afraid, Jenny. I'm afraid of feeling how you did. I'm afraid that you won't be there to help me. Most of all, I'm afraid of never seeing him ever again and I don't know how I can *be* if that happens.

But also I don't know how it can be any other way. It's inevitable, like a trap closing on me with its jagged steel jaws about to tear me apart. I watch the hinge closing on me in slow motion and soon it will rip into me.

I am afraid to hurt so much.

CHAPTER 34

There's no news from you in the morning. Sleep came to claim me eventually at around 5 a.m. When I finally drag myself out of bed, I go to find Harry at the cottage.

'Sorry, rough night.'

'Thinking about your sister?'

'Yeah.'

'How do you feel now?'

'Hungry. I missed breakfast, but OK otherwise.'

He smiles. 'I can fix that.'

He makes me breakfast and I wolf it down. When I'm with him like this, the 2 a.m. fears seem ridiculous.

'I didn't do much work with Merlin before.'

'How come?'

'I was sort of worried about you. I couldn't really concentrate.'

'Sorry, I should have texted only I was zonked by then. I fell asleep just before I was due to get up and come downstairs. Which is so annoying because I'd been awake for hours before that.'

'No, it's fine. I was going to suggest a walk – we can take him with us and fly him somewhere he's not so familiar with.'

I push my empty plate away. 'I'm ready. Let's go.'

We walk out to Wolfscott Hill and I know that's where you used to walk a lot. It's where they did the search. There's hardly anybody about.

'It's always quiet in the morning,' Harry tells me.

The top of the hill is a broad, flat area with a ruined stone tower.

'It was a lookout point once,' Harry says.

'Why didn't they build the castle up here?'

'I think there was one here originally. My dad told me once. This hill is the highest thing for miles that's big enough to take a castle on its peak, but the original one was still quite small. When they wanted to expand in later years, times had changed and it wasn't so important to see an enemy coming from miles off like they needed to in Norman times. When they moved down the hill they wanted to be able to get everyone in from the surrounding villages in case they were attacked too. At least that's what Dad said. He was into all that stuff.'

As we look down the hill on the castle below and can see everything laid out beneath us, his dad's explanation makes sense. We stand for a while and gaze out over the fields and then Harry gets Merlin ready to fly.

'Go right over there, yes, there by that rock on the ground.'

I stand and wait as he walks off in the opposite direction, going far further than he normally does. He takes ages to release Merlin, messing around with the jesses that keep him tethered.

The hawk flies straight to my outstretched arm. There's no hesitation in his flight or in his landing. He is well used to this now and to me. I stroke his chest as he nibbles on his reward. It takes me a few seconds to notice the piece of paper tied to his leg. When I remove it, curled up like a little scroll, I look up to see Harry watching me, his arms folded across his chest.

I open the paper with some difficulty, only having one hand because Merlin's still perched on the other.

'I love you,' it says.

It is the most perfect way he can tell me because it is perfectly him. I place a kiss on the note and slip it safely in my pocket, knowing he'll see this and understand my answer.

He comes over and retrieves Merlin, then takes hold of my

hand and we walk down the hill together. And I understand that Merlin didn't really need more exercise at all. We don't talk on the way down the hill, but we don't let go of each other's hands.

Harry puts Merlin out on his perch when we get back to the cottage and makes coffee.

This is what he does to me – he makes the quiet moments of life so alive. Moments like these have become more to me than any other. He hands me a mug and we stand watching Merlin together.

'He's ready to fly displays, I think,' Harry says and there is a quiet pride in his voice.

'But you won't fly him at the Wolfscott displays?'

'No, I'll try him at some local events to start off with. See how he goes – it'll give me a feel for how it would be to build that up into a business.'

He's really thought this through. 'You can make a living out of it then?'

'If you can get bookings for events, but you also need to be able to do individual sessions and train other people to handle the birds. I need to build that area up more before I cut loose from here completely. But I'll get there.'

But I won't be here to see that. I hear the words in my head, but don't say them.

To erase the thought, I place our coffee mugs on the ground

and wind my arms round his neck and kiss him. His arms are tight around me and his lips are on mine and there is nothing in the world but us and now.

CHAPTER 35

My phone bleeps. I dive over the bed to grab it from the cabinet.

Meet me at Strawlins Point 2 p.m. Don't tell anyone.

I stare, dumbfounded, and then burst into hot, noisy tears. You're ready to see me.

I check my watch: 10 a.m. Then I realise I don't have a clue where or what Strawlins Point is. I scrabble in the drawer for the hotel's information pack, which has maps in it. In four hours I'm going to see you. Just four hours.

I scan the maps and begin to panic because I can't see anything called Strawlins Point.

Calm. Focus. Study the maps.

Strawlins Point. It sounds like somewhere high up. I go over the maps more carefully, refusing to let myself get stressed.

And there on the second map, among the woods to the east, I find a spot called Strawlins Point. It appears to be a clearing in the trees at the top of a ridge of hills. There's one winding path that leads to the top. I estimate the distance. It looks around three miles from here and steeply uphill so I need to leave about an hour and a half to get there. I'll leave at noon, to be sure.

I'm supposed to meet Harry for lunch, but this is more important. I'll leave him a note on one of the cages.

So two whole hours before I can set out to see you. What can I do?

I can text you back. I should have thought about that straight away.

Will be there. Missed you so much. Love you xoxoxoxoxo

I've waited weeks for this.

I scribble a note for Harry: *Something's come up and had to go out. Will see you later <3 H*

I sit down to memorise the route. I'll take the map with me, of course, but this will help me to get there quicker . . .

But my methodical approach isn't working. I've gone into a complete tailspin. Dad's gone into town. Did you know that somehow? Or is that a coincidence? I pace up and down my room until I think I'll wear a hole in the carpet.

The day before you came to England we sat up in the tree house for the last time together. You lay on the floor, staring up at the rafters, and I sat in the doorway, swinging my legs.

'It's going to be amazing, Hannah. I just know it is. This feels like my life is really starting. All the things I've talked about and dreamed about, they're all finally beginning to happen. In less than forty-eight hours I'm going to be in England.'

'I wish I could come too.'

'Maybe you can come visit when I go over there for good.'

'Is that what you're going to do?'

'Maybe. I've been doing some research. There are some amazing schools in London where you can learn to be a nanny, at college level. If this job works out, maybe I could ask Mom and Dad about doing something like that.'

'So you want to go forever?' I asked in a small voice.

'Not necessarily. I'd like to go to school there and then maybe I could come back here and work, or I could travel. Lots of nannies do that – work for families who travel a lot. Like I could get a job in the US, but with a family who go around the world, you know, maybe the mom and dad have to do that for their work.'

'Oh yeah, that'd be cool. We'd still see you.'

'Before you know it, you'll be making plans too. You won't want to stay here forever, Hannah.'

'I'm not like you though. I don't know what I want.'

'You've got plenty of time to decide. You'll work it out.' You traced circles in the dust on the floor. 'You can be anything you want. You're much smarter in school than me. There is so much out there in the world, so much to do and see. That's what scares me – a lifetime isn't enough. Just exploring England could take me that long.'

I envied you that day for being the first one to set her feet on that path, while I had to wait behind. Always waiting to follow you – that's the fate of the younger sister. Never first, never in pole position, always the follower.

You giggled. 'I've been making a list of all the things in England I want to see since I was ten years old. It's going to be epic, Hannah!'

I shake my head. Epic. The last few weeks have been pretty epic, but not in the way you meant. I look at the clock and finally it's time to go.

The walk up through the trees is probably beautiful, but I'm too distracted to appreciate it. The path is all dappled light from the canopy of oak and beech leaves above. As the hill climbs higher, the trees around me change to a rowan and birch mix and there are the beginnings of berries appearing among the feathery leaves of the rowan. After a while I have to concentrate on the track, which gets narrower, stonier and steeper with some tricky bits. It's nothing to some of the trails we've walked together, but I have to watch my step all the same.

I'm sweating by the time I reach the clearing at the top. There's a stone structure in the centre with wooden boards on top and a bench by the side. I sit down, my legs protesting at the sudden stop. I check my phone. Fifteen minutes to wait.

Or are you here already? There's only one path up here after all. Did you come early so we wouldn't meet on the way? And why did you choose this isolated spot anyway?

I look around, but there's no sign of you and no messages on my phone. I sigh and settle back to wait. I read the plaque attached to the stone wall.

Strawlins Well is a natural borehole that has been used for centuries as a source of fresh water. The well fell out of use in the 1920s when the land was no longer grazed and was planted with trees. Strawlins Well and Strawlins Point are maintained by the Cheshire Wildlife Trust within an area of high biodiversity.

Then my phone vibrates.

Look under the bench.

I slam my phone down and look under my feet in a rush of irritation. This cryptic business is really grating on my nerves.

Nothing.

So I get on my knees and crawl underneath the bench. Then I see it. Taped to the underside are a note and a wrench. I tear the note off.

Open the cover.

Open the cover of what? I get up, holding the wrench, and look around. The only thing here is that well. Then I notice the bolts holding the cover down. They should be rusty with disuse.

But they're not — they're shiny and gleaming like someone has oiled them recently.

I stop and look around and listen. Not a sound. Nothing. I place the wrench on one of the bolts and give a half-hearted turn to see if it moves. It does, easily. I unscrew it and then work my way around the other four. When I give the wooden cover a shove, I discover it's in two halves and I lift one flap back on to the other.

There's another note pinned to the lid. I'm getting really mad with this, Jenny. Mad and scared. I rip the note off.

Here lies Jenny Tooley in her final resting place.

My vision bleaches out . . .

. . . What? . . .

I hear myself scream as if from a distance and the earth seems to drop away under my feet.

CHAPTER 36

When I peeled my face away from the cold stone of the hillside, I called the cops, and then I called Dad. I don't think I was making much sense and they told me to stay exactly where I was. There was no danger of me leaving you, so that was a pointless instruction. The cops scrambled a chopper to get out to me and make sure I was safe until they could get officers on the ground up there. All the time I held on to the stones of the well, as if in doing so I could hold on to you.

I knew that last note was true, knew it in my bones as if they recognised you were close.

Dad pulled me away when he arrived with the cops. I pointed at the phone and the notes and then buried my head in Dad's chest.

'She's dead,' I said and that was all I could say, over and over again.

He stroked my back and cried into my hair while the cops did their work around us.

It was awful. They had to send a special caving team down to find you. They wanted us to return to the hotel, but I wouldn't go. I'd have fought anyone who tried to make me. So they put up an incident tent around the well and made us sit off to one side. Hot tea was brought up to us in a flask. I don't know how many hours we sat there waiting, Dad and I, holding on to each other, but eventually an officer came over to us.

'I'm sorry, sir, miss, but we think we've found Jenny.'

Dad got up and pushed me away and ran into the trees. We heard him vomiting.

'I'm so sorry,' the officer said, staring helplessly after Dad.

Coombs arrived and curtly sent him back to his duties and then he went after Dad. I'm glad it was him. After a while he came back with his arm resting over Dad's shoulders, kind of like they were buddies, but really it was to help Dad hold it together.

'Can I see her?' I asked him.

Coombs shook his head. 'Not until she's been identified, and then it's up to your dad.'

'I'll do it now,' Dad said. 'I want to see her. Is she recognisable?'

'She is,' Coombs said in his most professional voice. 'She's been in the water down there and she's in a condition where she can be identified. The water is very cold and mineralised from the stone and that has –' I guess he stopped because even he wasn't quite sure how to say she's not decomposed without making the bile rise in our throats again.

'I want to see her now. I need to tell her something. Can we do that, please?' Dad squared his shoulders.

'You know we can do it in more suitable conditions?'

'I want to do it now. She's been alone without us long enough.'

Coombs nodded. 'There's one other thing then. We found another body. Unlike Jenny, this girl's body was caught on a rock and didn't land in the water so it's not so well preserved. I didn't want it to come as a surprise when you enter the tent and see two body bags.'

'Is it Cassie?' I asked.

'We believe it may be, but there will need to be formal identification.'

Poor Cassie. Definitely murder then.

Of course it was murder. You couldn't have bolted yourself in the well, but I'd had a brief, stupid moment of wondering if you'd killed yourself.

I couldn't fully take it all in though . . . It felt like a nightmare, not quite reality yet.

'How long has Jenny been there?'

'Forensics will have to do more before they can confirm, but it seems likely she's been there since the time she went missing.'

From the very beginning.

So the texts . . . they weren't from you.

That means someone had your phone. And that all this time, the texts have been from the person who killed you. The whole time someone's been playing with me. As I understand that, a wave of nausea passes through me.

'One final thing before I take you over there,' Coombs added. 'We found a small rucksack beside Jenny. It contains her purse with some photos of the family. And also a zip wallet stuffed with banknotes.'

'The money from the account?' Dad asked.

'It looks that way.'

'So whoever killed her didn't take it or didn't find it?'

'It was easy to find. Whatever the motivation was, it wasn't money.'

Somehow this made it worse.

Dad went with Coombs. 'Can I see her too?' I called to him.

He waved at me to wait and I shuffled from foot to foot until he reappeared and came for me. 'It's OK. You can come if you want.' I guess he had to check for himself if Coombs was right and you were still . . . I don't know . . . intact . . . not rotted away . . .

Even thinking those words was a horror beyond horrors.

Dad held my hand as we went into the tent. There were a few officers in there at a respectful distance from your body, and then I noticed behind their feet lay another body, shrouded in a bag. They were masking poor Cassie from us.

Your bag was open. Your face looked out at us, but your eyes were closed. You looked like a sleeping mermaid, your hair in wet fronds around you. There was not a mark on your face, but a ring of ugly bruises disfigured your neck. You were pale and you were still beautiful.

You were still Jenny.

I had tears, Jenny. Tears I couldn't stop, no matter how many people were there to watch me.

Dad knelt beside you and kissed your forehead, like he used to do when we were little girls and he tucked us up in bed.

'I love you, sweetheart,' he said. 'Forever. We'll take you home and you can sleep in peace.'

You'd be cold. I knew that when I knelt beside him, but I didn't know how cold until I touched your hand. I almost recoiled, but I was looking at your face and you were too much Jenny for me to do that. I wrapped my little finger around yours. 'Always,' I said. It was enough. You would know.

We waited there a while, me pinky swearing with you and Dad stroking your hair until Coombs came and put his arm round Dad's shoulders again and said, 'It's time to go.'

Dad nodded and stood up, half-lifting me with him because there was no strength in my knees to hold me. We stumbled from the tent. They gave us more tea before they brought us down the hill. You would be airlifted out on a stretcher. A car drove us back to Wolfscott.

'What now?' Dad said brokenly to Coombs as he got out of the car.

'This is a murder investigation,' Coombs replied. 'Please be careful who you talk to here. I must ask you not to discuss the case. We'll say more about that in the morning, but please, for now say nothing about it. Tell them there's an embargo on you speaking about it. I'd like you to consider moving to another hotel if that's possible. I know the Cadwalladers have been very hospitable, but we are dealing with an entirely different situation now.'

'You think it could be someone here.'

'We need to consider all possibilities. She may have known her killer.'

His words sent a tremor running down my spine and I looked around convulsively to see if we were being watched, but it was too dark to see anything.

He walked us into the hotel. Mrs Cadwallader came rushing towards us with a question dying on her lips as she saw Coombs behind us. I guess from our faces she had her answer anyway.

'No questions, please,' said Coombs. 'I think these people

need to get to their rooms. Perhaps you could send some food up for them.'

'Oh . . . er . . . yes, certainly. Um, yes, do go up and I'll organise a tray.'

We didn't wait to be asked what we wanted. We just trudged past her and up the stairs. I followed Dad into his room and we sank down into the chairs.

'I need to call Mom,' he said suddenly. 'Oh God, what will I say to her?'

'I don't know,' I said, curling myself into a ball on the chair. Heartbreak feels a lot like stomach ache when the shock passes off and you're left an empty, shocked shell.

'You go take a hot bath, honey. I'll run one for you and get your pyjamas. Then I'll call Mom.'

'Can I speak to her?'

'Let me talk to her first. Then I'm going to call Maria from next door to go round and see if she needs help with Brandon.'

I sank into the hot bath he ran for me. And then I heard him on the phone to Mom.

'Baby, I need you to be strong. I've got news and it's not good.' His voice cracked. 'It's the worst news it could be.'

There was a pause.

'Yes, she's dead.'

And another pause.

I slid my head under the water to block it out. I didn't want to hear any more. When I came up, he was saying goodbye to Mom and crying worse so I put my head under again.

When it was finally safe to get out, my fingers and toes were wrinkled. I rubbed my hair as dry as I could with a towel, put my pyjamas on and went through. There were sandwiches, cake and hot chocolate on a tray. 'You must eat something, Hannah,' Dad said firmly. 'I know you don't want to. I don't either. But we need to be strong for your mom, for each other and most of all for Jenny because she'd want that.'

So I ate mechanically until I could get away with saying I'd had enough. Dad looked so tired and old, sitting there chewing on a sandwich that I knew he wasn't tasting.

'You should go to bed,' he said. 'You look tired out.' He walked me the short distance down the corridor to my room and kissed me goodnight. 'Make sure the door is locked.'

'I will.'

I keep the light on as I get in the bed. I can't stand to turn it off yet. I need to go through all this before I forget how it felt. I owe that to you, to capture it just as it was.

Before we found your body, I couldn't believe you could be gone. Not a real and true belief. I never could give in. Now that hope's been taken away and there is nothing inside me but anger and hate for whoever did this to you. It's a tiny flame at first, but as I sit here alone in the silence, I come to understand

just what you being dead means for all of us, and most of all for you because now you'll never get to see all those places you wanted to. Never get to love and never get to have your own children. And you would have made the most amazing mom in the world.

Now I come to understand all this, that tiny flame stokes up to a fire. It burns hot and fierce and I will find out who did this to you and, if I can, I will kill them, Jenny. There is no forgiveness in me for whoever did this and there never will be.

The firecracker, Dad calls me. What that means is that I can be as driven by anger as you are by love and right now I'm as mad as hell. I won't be anything else until he . . . she . . . whoever it is . . . is dead. And I want it to be a death that's as slow and painful as anybody can make it.

I will make sure that you aren't forgotten and that whoever killed you pays. Something has changed within me, Jenny. Something is broken forever. All the time on CNN I see news stories of people being killed, hurt, sometimes by the ones they love and sometimes by strangers, and it seems like it happens so often that you don't stop to question it. Bad things happen; that's how the world is.

But when it happens to someone you love, it calls into question everything you ever knew or thought. How can there be a world in which this happens to someone like you? What sickness is inside a person's head to make them put their hands around your throat and take you from us? I do not know how to even comprehend that.

I hear the softest of taps at my door and then a whisper, 'Hannah?'

It's Harry.

In all of this, I haven't thought of him once, but hearing his voice, I get this rush of relief, of something so opposite to the despair of a second ago. And I'm overwhelmed with guilt that I can allow myself to feel that way.

I pad over and open the door. His eyes scan my face anxiously. They are the eyes I need to see. Eyes that don't reside in a world where good and beautiful sisters get killed. Eyes that don't understand how that can be either.

'She's dead, isn't she?' he whispers.

I nod and he puts his arms around me and closes the door behind us. He leads me over to the bed and kicks off his shoes. He draws me down beside him and turns out the bedside light. I try to speak, but he puts his finger to my lips and pulls the duvet over us. Then he wraps his arms around me and rests his face against my hair.

'Sshh,' he says and presses a soft kiss behind my ear.

My brain is too confused, too drained, too lost without you to think any longer and so I sleep in the circle of Harry's arms.

CHAPTER 37

When I wake in the morning, Harry is still there. I've turned in my sleep and my face is tucked into his neck. He's still asleep and I study his face. It's a luxury that I can't have when he's awake.

He has the straightest eyebrows. I want to trace the line of them, but I'm afraid to wake him. His eyelashes look much longer with his eyes closed, a dark, protective fringe keeping him safe inside sleep. I wish I was still there with him. I slept a deep, dreamless sleep last night, but I wake to a future without you in it.

What will I do now, Jenny? Who will I be without you to follow after?

'You OK?' Harry says thickly as his eyelids drift open and he finds me watching him, although I'm no longer seeing his face.

I rub my eyes – they're stinging with tears and he can see them. 'I need a shower,' I say, sitting up.

'I should go. I don't think your dad would like to find me here.' He pulls me close and kisses me on the mouth. There are different kinds of kisses, I am learning. There are kisses with passion and kisses that say simply, 'I'm here for you.' The latter is what I need right now and he knows that. 'What happens today?'

'I'm not supposed to talk about it. We're going to the police station.'

'Then I won't ask. Will I see you later?'

'I'll call you.'

'OK.' He gives me a last kiss and slips out of my room.

I feel cold and chilled through without him so I go into the shower and turn the hot water up as high as I can and batter myself with the jets. I dress quickly and throw on some jeans and a shirt. It's the clothing equivalent of comfort food. Then I go in search of Dad. He's up and ready too.

'I asked them to bring breakfast up here,' he says. 'The police are collecting us at 8.30.'

'What's going to happen now, Dad?'

'I talked to Mom and I'm going to stay here until they release Jenny, then I'm going to bring her home.' His eyes are awash with tears before he gets even halfway through that statement and he stands up abruptly. I hear him in the bathroom blowing his nose and when he comes back he's holding it together again. 'Mom and I both think you should go back home now. You need your mom and she needs you. It's not good for you here.'

'No! I'm not leaving! I'll go back when Jenny goes back. Besides, I want whoever did this caught.'

'So do I, honey. But I also want you safe and one other girl has died already. I want you to go home.'

I shake my head. 'I'm not going without her. I promised her I'd see this through and I'm not breaking that promise. You can't ask me to!'

'You could be in danger here. That's more important. There's some crazy person around here killing girls and I want you far away from that.'

'Let's see what the cops say. Please?'

He shakes his head at me. 'I don't know where you get your stubbornness from. We'll speak to the police but don't think that's going to change my mind.'

It's not that I don't want to go home and see Mom and Brandon. Part of me wants that more than anything else in the world, but I promised you and there's nothing more I can do for you now than keep that promise. I think the promises we make to the dead must be the most binding of all because we can never make it up to them if we break those.

I don't even consider Harry in all of this. I don't allow

myself to. You are what's important here and I can't let myself forget that.

I see Tom on our way downstairs. He is carrying a tray of glasses to the bar. He looks up and sees me, and his face registers our presence with a flood of feelings across it. He stops in his tracks, his eyes trying to send me his sorrow from across the length of the lobby. 'I am so sorry,' he mouths at me. 'So sorry.' His mouth trembles with suppressed emotion.

CHAPTER 38

I am sick of the inside of this police station. Its white walls have aged to a miserable nearly grey and I never want to be here again. Until the day they catch the person who killed you, that is – I could put up with it then. I could put up with most places to hear that news.

We're given that horrible coffee again. Coombs is back on duty, heavy-eyed as if he worked late last night. 'I hoped we'd be meeting in happier circumstances,' he says as we sit down around a table. 'I know I might not always have given that impression, but I wanted to believe we'd find her alive.'

'Thank you for everything you've done,' Dad replies.

He shakes his head. 'I did my job. Sometimes my job isn't a pleasant one at all. I have a little girl myself.'

Out of nowhere, Dad holds out his hand and Coombs shakes it. 'I hope that little girl always stays as safe as it's possible to be. I hope the worst thing that ever happens to her is a cut knee. I really mean that.' He takes a deep breath. 'So what happens now? There's forensics, right?'

'Yes. Please forgive them for taking their time, but they'll want to gather any possible evidence that could be used to find and incriminate whoever did this to Jenny, and to Cassie Evans.'

'It was Cassie then?' I interrupt.

'It was. She was identified this morning.'

'Why? Why would anyone do this?'

Coombs looks at me with what can only be described as the infinite sadness of someone who has seen too much and still doesn't understand any of it. And I appreciate that he can't answer my question because there is no answer a sane and rational human being can give. When you meet evil, it just cannot be understood.

'What I need to make clear now is that everyone is a suspect. Initial examination suggests Jenny was killed soon after she disappeared and we're waiting for forensics to confirm the exact timing. We need to examine the content of those texts again and look at the new ones. There could be something important there that might provide us with a clue. We've still not been able to trace who Jenny was with the day she withdrew that money, but we don't believe it was Cassie. There's enough CCTV images to compare and we do think that it was most likely a man. Both girls are tall, but an analysis of the unidentified person's build tells us it's probably male. While we mustn't leap to conclusions, that person is now a key suspect who we need most urgently to trace. Once an announcement is made to the press, we'll be releasing details of that CCTV footage.'

'So when Cassie said Jenny might be seeing someone, that person could be the one who killed them,' I say slowly, thinking it through, trying to get a handle on whether there were any more clues at all in what Cassie said. But I'd been through this so many times already and come up with nothing.

'Whoever that was is a prime suspect. If Jenny had been seeing someone they haven't come forward, so an innocent explanation is unlikely by this point. Has there been any further attempt to contact you, Hannah?'

'No.' A shiver runs through me at the thought that he or she or whoever might try to contact me now.

'I do think that the perpetrator will attempt contact again. It's likely that he, or she, will text you. This individual seems to like mind games. It's essential you let us know immediately should that happen because it could be the breakthrough we need.'

I glare at Dad and he knows exactly what I mean and I

211

know exactly what he was planning on saying. He was about to tell Coombs he's sending me home. After what I just heard, he'll have to drug me and tie me up to get me on a plane. If these guys think the messages could be the key to Jenny's killer being caught, then I'm staying right here and nobody is going to stop me.

'What kind of person does this?' Dad asks.

'I've had Heather working on that and she's been on it most of the night.'

'OK,' Dad braces himself. 'I need to hear this so tell me.'

'She feels the most likely option is that we're dealing with a psychopath. Now forget everything you've heard in films and on TV: what we're talking about is someone who lacks all remorse and empathy, who feels only on a superficial level. A psychopath in a very real sense might not care if you live or die. Their brains even look different on a scan – keeping it simple, they're wired differently to the rest of us. They are so emotionally disconnected that they can see people as objects to be manipulated or destroyed without any compunction. In extreme cases, they can kill without conscience and may even take pleasure in doing so. We thinks it's highly likely that the killer was up on the hill yesterday watching as you found the bodies. That person may even have been there when we arrived. They will have derived satisfaction from doing that, in Heather's professional opinion, and will have wanted to see the consequences of what they've done.'

I shudder. 'And you think Jenny would be seeing someone or even be friends with a weirdo like that? Then you don't know a thing about her.'

'No, here's the thing,' says Coombs patiently. 'It's very difficult to spot them in society. They're often extremely good at masking themselves. They can be very adept at understanding your emotions, but they don't feel those emotions themselves and they don't care. It makes them great manipulators. They can convince you that they are charming and funny, some of the nicest people you could ever meet if it suits their purposes. But they're playing a game with you.'

The blood leaves my face, Dad's too, for I see him pale. 'So it could be anyone?'

'Exactly. Which is why I need you to understand that everyone has to be a suspect until eliminated. It is crucial that you take this on board. It is very likely, according to Heather, that Jenny knew her killer well. Probably Cassie too. There's still this business of the bank account unresolved too. Was Jenny with her killer the day she took that money out?'

'That would mean it's most likely to be someone at Wolfscott then!'

'Yes, it could be.'

'We're leaving now!' Dad stands up, pushing the table back. 'I need to find us a hotel.'

'No, Dad. That might wreck everything. It might make them suspicious and –'

'Hannah, if you seriously think I'm going to spend another night in the same place as the lunatic freak who murdered my daughter . . . and if you think for a second that I'll expose you to that –'

'I would advise moving,' Coombs cuts in. 'We certainly don't want either of you in danger.'

Dad slams his hand on the table so hard I think the legs will break. 'Danger! I won't be in any danger! When I find out who he is, I'll kill him with my bare hands. You tell me that some maniac killed my baby and he enjoyed it . . .' He stares around wildly at all of us and then his face crumples. He slumps on the table, his head in his hands, howling in rage and pain.

A policewoman comes and leads me away. 'You let DI Coombs have a chat with him, love,' she says. 'Come with me to the canteen and I'll get you a hot chocolate and a bun.' I should hate her for thinking hot chocolate and cake could make up for the loss of you, but it's what Mom would have done and I start to cry because she's not here now with me and I need her so badly.

I sniffle into my hot chocolate and the woman gets me a tissue. 'I want to call my mom,' I tell her. It's more a wail than speech.

'Sit here then,' she says, 'and I'll go and arrange something for you.'

It's probably only ten minutes before she comes back, but it feels like a lot longer. They put me in a small office with the phone and they're not supposed to leave me, but the woman waits outside with the door only a little ajar.

'Mom?'

'Hannah, baby . . .' And Mom starts crying. Which I guess people might think would make me feel worse, but it doesn't because what other response is normal from our mom when you're dead, Jenny?

'Mom, I miss you so much.' I'm crying again too.

'I wish I could be there, baby. I wish I could come. Dad and I want you to come home right away, Hannah. Has he told you that?'

'Yeah, but I can't. I can't leave her. I made her a promise.' I know I won't need to say more. Mom will understand that. I can tell from how she sobs harder that she does. 'Please, Mom, you have to make Dad understand. He's . . . he's not coping that well right now. If I can get him, can you be here to talk to him, please?'

The policewoman fetches him for me and I talk to Mom while we wait. Stupid stuff like how Brandon wanted pancakes for breakfast and how we've run out of syrup.

I don't know what Mom and Dad talk about on the phone, but I know when Dad comes out he's calmer, like some of the anger is locked away. I know it can't be gone. I know that because I feel inside myself how it isn't gone at all — just held back in there.

We ride back to Wolfscott in the car to pack because Dad says he's taking the first hotel he can find to get us out of there, even if it's a fleapit.

So I have to find out quickly, before they say you're ready to come home, who did this to you. I wish you could hear me. I wish you could speak and give me a clue. If you could be a ghost, Jenny, I'd want you to haunt me forever, but right now I'd settle for ten minutes so you could tell me who it was.

I pin a note to the owl cage. There's no sign of Harry, but from the number of birds missing it looks like there's a demonstration on so his phone will be turned off. The note says we had to leave and I'll call him later.

The Cadwalladers hurry into reception just as we're leaving. 'What . . . ?' Mr Cadwallader says.

'We need to leave,' Dad says firmly. 'Police instructions. I'm sure they'll explain.'

'But —'

'Two girls from here are dead, dammit! I'm not risking my other daughter by staying another second in this place.'

Mrs Cadwallader glances nervously up the stairs where two guests have stopped, open-mouthed, to listen.

Dad casts her a contemptuous glance. 'You need to get your

house in order, not worry about what your guests overhear. You've got some maniac loose in this place, killing young girls. God help you all if you don't take that seriously. Now I thank you for your hospitality, but we need to go. Come on, Hannah.'

As we drive away, his knuckles are white and clenched in anger. 'You shouldn't have said that, Dad. The police said –'

'I know, Hannah, I know.'

CHAPTER 39

The new hotel isn't exactly a fleapit, but it's nothing like Wolfscott either. It's situated about five miles away off a main road and most of the other guests seem to be people on a walking holiday. The whole place smells of boots and waterproofs and damp dogs. Dad goes to organise a rental car and then goes for a walk to clear his head. I lie on the bed.

I can't grieve until I've had vengeance and I can't get vengeance by sitting around crying for you. I know it'll be anger that pulls me through the tough stuff. I'm easy with that. Anger and I are old friends. But anger without logic is a nuclear bomb and I need a targeted missile. I need a plan.

What was it exactly that Cassie said? I try to remember her words.

I've just been wondering over the past few days whether it's possible she could have been seeing someone she hadn't told me about.

. . . I'm not sure really. I mean, I'm not even sure I do think it. I just can't think of any other reason why she could have disappeared like this . . .

. . . Maybe a couple of small things like we seemed to spend a bit less time together over the last month than before. She seemed a bit preoccupied at times. Once, when we talked about the end of the season and me going away and her going home, she didn't seem like she was looking forward to it as much as she had before. Just little things that probably add up to nothing.

Try as I might, I just couldn't find a clue in any of that.

Except that . . . Wait! Of course, that was it!

I've been so stupid. The very fact that you kept it so hidden from me, from Cassie — that's a clue in itself. This wasn't you wanting to keep yourself to yourself. That's my kind of trick, not yours. You had to keep quiet about it for a reason. OK, so that isn't telling me who the guy is, but this is progress. I can work with this.

I leap off the bed and scrabble in my luggage for a notebook and a pen.

Reasons to tell no one:

1. He's married or in a relationship.

That's the most obvious, of course. That's the reason anyone would keep it hidden. And . . . and it makes it likely that Cassie knew him! Would know he wasn't single.

I chew the end of the pen.

2. It's someone we wouldn't like.

It's a possible and I can see you keeping that from Cassie, but from me not so much. It's not like I ever pretended I liked Trey. Or maybe you didn't want to hear it from me again.

Ah, but maybe . . .

3. It's someone who didn't feel the same way about you.

Steve the falconer – you guys talked a lot; he's a married guy; you've been to his house and his wife didn't know about it.

Mr Cadwallader – married and if it was him you totally couldn't tell anyone; also he can be charming, but he has a darker side according to what I've been told.

Aubrey the chef – he has a girlfriend and him having a prison record might be another reason not to tell anyone.

Michael the waiter, who'd been helping you search online to find family.

Oh God, another reason that could fit then . . .

4. You didn't tell us because you weren't interested, but he was obsessed with you and you didn't know how much.

That could fit Michael. Maybe. He could have been quietly fixated on you and no one knew.

This is hopeless. There are so many staff in Wolfscott and I know only a handful. And I'm clutching at straws here.

Oliver, the driver – he might have had a thing about

you and he creeps out all the girls, including me.

Tom – who isn't into younger girls.

Harry – . . .

I stop. Surely, that's just ridiculous. But I need to check off everyone I know.

Harry – who . . . is younger than you so you were embarrassed . . . or who was into you and you didn't feel the same . . .

Of course it can't be Harry. Even the idea makes me feel like throwing up. Harry isn't like that at all. There's no violence or hate in Harry. But Coombs said they hide all of that, these people who kill without conscience. *I* would know though. I would know if Harry was one of them. He's not – Harry loves me.

I shiver. What if Harry was drawn to me because I'm like you? I was suspicious of him at first . . .

This is so wrong – it cannot, *cannot* be him.

Psychopaths like playing games with you, Coombs told us that. Making me love him after he killed you, well, that could be the biggest game of all.

I am as cold as if I was drowning in the Arctic Ocean. But I have to work this out.

Do the thing you fear most first, that's what they say. Dad's always telling me that. He's says it's got him where he is in business. And as Harry is what I fear most now, he's the person

I have to investigate first. I cannot talk myself out of that because it's him. I have to be objective, like Coombs will be, and Coombs will investigate everybody. His mind will be open just as I'm going to force mine to be.

So to set a trap I need to consider the evidence carefully. I need to know what kind of monster I could be dealing with because I can't just sit here and do nothing. I can't!

Oh, Harry, it can't be you ... please, no ...

Jenny, you deserve no less. There is no room for sentiment. To fight this kind of monster I need blood as cold as his. I must be prepared for the unthinkable.

I need to pay Harry a visit. I don't know how I'm going to evade Dad or how I'm going to get there, but I have to see him, try to get him to slip up. Or prove himself innocent.

And all the time I'm thinking this, my heart is being torn to pieces like his birds shred their bait.

CHAPTER 40

In the next few hours, I learn more on Google about psychopaths than I ever wanted to know. One of the signs Coombs didn't mention when he spoke to us was an admiration for predators, a respect for the pitilessness of their killing. It's the call of like to like, the article said. The psychopath recognises the killer without a conscience in the animal world and he understands that in a mirror image of the way he fails to understand why the human race cares about hurting others. There is no empathy in a predator for its prey and with those creatures the psychopath feels at home and perhaps understood by them for the first time in his life.

I think of Harry and the birds, and a little bit more of my heart is shredded.

I read on, and as I do, I get more and more scared. 'The psychopath you fall in love with' is the next article I come across. It backs up what Coombs said, but goes further. A psychopath can make you believe he's in love with you and he will do anything to get what he wants. And he'll do that by reading what you want in those early days and supplying it. If you want excitement, he'll give you that. If you need a shoulder to lean on, he'll give you that too.

Is that what happened? Harry became what I needed to get through the hell of you being missing? I don't want to believe it, and yet . . .

The simplest solutions are the best. I tell Dad I have a headache and I'm going to bed early, then I sneak out and call a taxi. I've got ten missed calls from Harry. I turned voicemail off so he couldn't leave a message.

When I get to the gates at Wolfscott, I call him back. I'm shaking, but I have to do this – I'm the only one who can set this particular trap. I'm taking the biggest risk of my life, but I keep telling myself that this is for you. I'll stay smart: I won't let him know what I'm up to. It's pouring with rain, but I don't care.

'I need to see you.'

'Hannah, it's half ten. Where are you?'

'At the gate.'

'Wolfscott? Are you crazy? I'll come and get you.'

'I'll come to you. Are you home?'

'Yes. What, no! You can't walk here in the dark. Stay there –'

But I end the call and start walking to his cottage. He meets me when I'm not even halfway there. He's jogging down the path with a flashlight.

'Hannah, what are you doing?'

'I needed to see you.'

'I want to see you too, but –'

'Let's go to the cottage. I'll talk to you there.'

'OK,' he says in a puzzled, miserable voice. He takes my hand in his. Strong fingers. Fingers that make me feel safe. Fingers strong enough to choke my sister?

We walk to his cottage in silence. It's cold and I'm chilled from walking in the rain. When we arrive, I'm relieved to see he's got the log burner fired up. I go to sit beside it and steam rises up off my clothes.

'Take your coat off. I'll find you something dry to put on.' He goes off into the bedroom. I hang my coat on a wooden chair and push it closer to the stove.

He returns with some jeans and a sweater. 'Here. Stay by the fire. I'll wait in there till you're done.'

I scramble into the dry clothes quickly and call to him. He takes the wet stuff from me and throws it into the washer-dryer in the kitchenette. I hear the kettle click on as I sit down by the fire again and he makes some of that instant hot chocolate he keeps here just for me.

Can a boy like this be a monster? Can a boy with eyes that look as if they understand pain so well be an emotionless killer?

Harry brings me the hot chocolate and kneels in front of me as I cup my hands around it. 'I know the police told you to leave the hotel. The whole estate is talking about it. They think the killer is here, don't they?'

I nod, not trusting my voice to speak.

He sighs heavily. 'Everyone knows about Cassie too. But why her? Is there any connection or is it a random psycho doing it?'

Those words. Why did he choose those words?

'I'm not allowed to talk about it.'

'Not even to me?' He stares up at me.

'Not to anyone.'

His eyes are bewildered and I want so much to believe he's innocent. Love does that, doesn't it? It makes us want to believe the best. I wonder if that's why they say love is blind.

'Am I a suspect, Hannah?'

'Everyone's a suspect.'

He looks at me so sadly, as if I've torn something inside him too, and I want to say I'm sorry and of course I know it can't be him, but the truth is I don't know that at all and I won't lie.

He nudges my hand gently, reminding me of the hot chocolate, and I sip it. It occurs to me that I shouldn't. It might

226

not be safe. If he's who Coombs says, he could have put anything in it. I could wake tied up or I could never wake up again and then Dad would be taking both his daughters home in bags.

I'm not afraid, Jenny. I'm too full of ice-cold anger to feel afraid. There's no room for fear, only vengeance. If I'm wrong though, how will he ever forgive me for thinking this of him?

I guess that will be the price I have to pay. Don't get me wrong, Jenny. I don't say that lightly. I say it because I must.

Time to bait the trap. I need him to confess or to give something away. My phone is set to voice-record mode in my pocket.

'They think Jenny was strangled. Cassie too.'

He looks up at me, eyes wide, waiting for me to go on.

'And it's likely they were both killed as soon as they went missing.'

He nods, still waiting.

'The thing is though, I've been getting texts from Jenny since she disappeared. That's why I was so sure she was alive.' I watch his face carefully.

He sits up a bit straighter, his face puzzled. 'But if she was killed straight away then you can't have been.' He doesn't look like he expected this at all. Is he such a good liar that I can't tell?

'The texts came from her phone.'

His forehead furrows up as if it's a problem he's trying to solve. 'Then the killer must have her phone.'

'Yes.' I still can't read anything unusual in his face.

'But why keep texting you? Is it so you think she's still alive? What did the texts say?'

'At first, they were about her being in trouble and needing me to come find her. I'd text back and there'd be days sometimes before she replied. Then they started to be about more personal stuff, about our family.'

'Like what?' He settles back, his arms looped over my knees, listening intently. Playing with me? Or trying to help?

'The texts talked about her trying to trace our English family. It made me think that's why she'd disappeared. Me and Mom had a big argument about it on the phone.'

He screws his face up in confusion. 'That's weird. Why would the killer want to text you about that?' Then he sits back again. 'But wait a minute! I'm sitting here, listening to you talk about what was in the texts, and what you're actually saying is whoever killed your sister sent you texts that made you come over to England and has been texting you ever since. Do you realise how much danger that puts you in?'

'Yeah.' Although until he said it just then, it hadn't struck me that those first texts, if they weren't from Jenny, had no other purpose than to get me here. A shiver runs down my spine.

He scowls and his mouth sets in a hard line. 'And I could be a suspect. That's what you just told me. If I am, Hannah, do you know how much danger you're putting yourself in right now?'

Is this it? Is this where he confesses? Or is he threatening me? The sudden shaft of fear that spears me could be due to him being right and I really am putting myself at risk here, or it could be fear that I'm about to lose everything I ever believed about him. I'm really not sure which it is. 'I guess.'

He stands up, glaring down at me. 'You *guess*? You walk in here with a murder suspect and you *guess*! What would your dad say? What would the police say if they knew you were here?' He whirls away, his face furious, and I flinch back.

Is he going to hit me?

He slams his fist on the table. 'It's a good job I'm not the killer because you just did the most unbelievably stupid thing imaginable in coming here. What are you going to do – work your way round every suspect on the list?'

My face gives me away.

'Hannah, don't be so stupid. This man has killed two girls. This is not a game.'

I stand up, suddenly furious too. 'I know that. Do you think seeing my sister's dead body was a game to me?'

We glower at each other across the room. I think he's going to slam the table again, but he walks swiftly over to me instead. I take a step back, but he grabs me and pulls me into a hug so tight that I have to brace myself to breathe. 'You stupid girl,' he mumbles into my neck, once again demonstrating his complete lack of ability to charm with words, which makes my heart knit back together just a little. 'You can't take risks like this. You need to be careful. If something happened to you, I'd –' He squeezes me tighter, so tight it's a bit painful, but if he's telling the truth now is probably the time to put up with it and not complain.

I'm still not sure of him. I've not seen anything to make me think he could be the killer, but neither have I seen anything to make me think he couldn't be. Except he's so useless with words that maybe I have hope.

The light above us flickers as he holds me and presses muffled kisses into my hair. And then it goes out and plunges us into darkness.

He curses. 'Another power cut.'

I stand frozen. 'Does this happen a lot?'

'Out here, yes, the power's always going off. The castle has its own backup generators. Hang on, it might come back on in a minute. It sometimes does.'

We wait silently. My heart is beating a little faster – I'm here in the dark with someone on a suspect list and it's, well, it's not good.

Harry curses again. 'I'll get a candle. This is why a log burner is a good thing. At least that still works.'

He pulls away from me and I hurriedly sit down again in front of the fire. At least that gives out some light to see by.

He opens the door of the stove and the flames lick up, hot and comforting, while he scrabbles around in the kitchenette for the candle. When he finds one, he sets it down on a low table beside me.

'I'll make you another drink and then you're going home,' he says, filling a pan with water. He puts the pan on a fold-out grate on the stove. 'I'm tempted to ring your dad to come and get you. That'd be the safest option.'

'You can't! He'll go crazy.'

'It's nothing you don't deserve,' he says, frowning at me.

'Aren't you mad at me for suspecting you?'

He shrugs. 'I'm mad at you for putting yourself in danger. I can't think beyond that right now.'

I watch the candle flame, how it flickers, how it grows then diminishes like a breath in and out. I have no idea what to do next.

A moth flies past me and its lace wings brush my cheek, making me jump. It circles the candle.

'Why do they do that?' I ask.

'Nobody knows,' Harry answers, watching it make its flight around the flame, getting closer. 'One theory is that they mistake the light for the moon and that's what they use to navigate by at night. But they fly too close. They can't fly too close to the moon so they don't understand artificial light. Which means they don't appreciate the danger.' He sighs. 'It's just another example of how humans have screwed things up for animals.'

He reaches out for the moth and I start to gasp for I think he's going to kill it, but instead he catches it safe in carefully cupped hands. He walks to the front door and opens it a crack. I see him open his hands in the moonlight and let the moth go. 'There, fly safe,' he says and closes the door again.

It's then I know for sure, Jenny. It's not Harry. Hands that care enough to save a moth don't crush the life from a girl's throat.

He takes the pan off the heat and makes me more hot chocolate.

A boy who understands that the innocence of moths makes it necessary for him to protect them . . . a boy like that is not a psychopathic killer.

I've been an idiot. Harry loves those birds because he loves animals, end of. He likes working them and watching them fly, and he understands their simplicity. He doesn't take pleasure in watching them kill. The moth shows me that.

Have I destroyed what we feel about each other by not knowing that from the start?

He sits in front of me again while I sip the chocolate.

'I know it's not you,' I tell him. 'I was an idiot ever to think it could be.'

'How do you know?'

'I saw it in the candle flame.' And I stick my tongue out a little at him, testing to see if he believes me.

He gives a little laugh. It's got some tension in it, but it's a laugh all the same. Better than a fist on the table.

'OK, there were three specific things that made me not rule you out. The first was that the police said the killer probably knew both Jenny and Cassie well, so that made it most likely that it was someone at Wolfscott. And they also said the person was probably a psychopath. I was so scared that I ignored all the things there that told me it couldn't be you.'

'You're going to have to explain that. I'm not even sure what a psychopath is, except somebody who kills people.'

'It's not quite like that.' And I repeat what Coombs told me and then what I'd read on the Internet.

At that point he bursts out laughing. 'You know, a lot of kids at school called me weird because of the birds and my own brother thinks it's abnormal, but that's the first time anyone's thought it made me a cold-blooded killer.'

'Oh, shut up!' I can feel myself blushing. 'The stupid thing is that another of the signs is cruelty, particularly when the psychopath is a child – cruelty to animals is a really early indicator. So is cruelty to other children, but the animal one – that's the biggie. There's other things, like not caring about risk and being really charming. None of that is you at all.'

He reaches up and hugs me, laughing properly now.

'I'm glad you don't find me charming.'

He holds me and I hold him back for the longest time, then he takes my face in his hands and kisses me. 'I love you,' he says between kisses. 'Please don't take any more risks. I'll do whatever I can to help, but you must be careful.'

My phone vibrates in my pocket. Uh-oh, maybe Dad has found out I'm not in my room. I pull a face at Harry and get the phone out. There's a message. My hands are shaking as I open it. Harry hangs over my shoulder to look at it too.

So now you know. I'm disappointed. I didn't think you'd run away so easily.

CHAPTER 41

Predictably, when Harry makes me call Dad to come get me, Dad goes wild. He drives straight over. We go to the gates to wait for him.

Dad slams the door of the hire car furiously as he gets out. He looks Harry up and down. 'So this is the boyfriend, is it?'

'Yeah, but Dad –'

'Well, at least one of you had the sense to know how much danger you're putting yourself in, Hannah!' He holds his hand out to Harry. 'Thank you for looking after her.'

I breathe again and Harry mumbles something about it being his privilege and shuffles his feet.

'In the car,' Dad snaps at me. No such courtesies for me then. I am definitely in trouble.

'I'm probably grounded until I'm fifty,' I whisper to Harry. 'I'll call you.'

'Better grounded than killed,' Harry says firmly, closing the door on me.

'I got another text,' I tell Dad as he pulls away from Wolfscott.

He curses, flashing me a quick horrified glance, but he has to keep his eyes on the road. 'What does it say?

I read it to him.

'He's watching us, Dad. He knows we left Wolfscott.'

'When did this arrive?'

'While I was with Harry, which rules him out. There's no way he could have sent it.'

'I should think not! Given you were alone with him.' He glares at me. 'Please tell me that's not why you went there, to confront . . .'

I hang my head.

'You did, didn't you? You know sometimes, Hannah, words fail me with you!' He looks like he wants to grab me and shake me. 'Do you think burying one of my girls isn't enough for me? Right, that is it. As soon as we get back to that hotel you give me your phone and you do not leave the hotel until we fly home. You want to see that boy to say goodbye then fine – he can come over. But you will not leave. Do I make myself clear? Good, then when we arrive you will go to your room and go to bed. I need to call the police.'

Yup, I'm grounded for life, and I may be a fighter, but even I recognise when to quit with my dad, so when we get back I leave my phone with him and creep off to my room.

The first thing I do is get my list out and cross Harry's name off. I've been really dumb, getting grounded like this. What I should have done was get together with Harry to examine my list. He knows a lot more of the staff at Wolfscott and we could have gone through suspects together. Maybe I can get him to come over tomorrow and we can do it then. Time's running out though. As soon as they're done with your autopsy, we'll be leaving, taking you home.

I can't even call Harry.

I have to do this one last thing for you, Jenny. I have to. I just wish I knew how.

All I can do is go through the suspects again and try to work out which of them might best match the texts. If you were trying to trace family, then you could have told anyone you were close to so it doesn't make any difference that Michael helped you find which British websites to use, or that Tom told me that you'd been intending to do that.

Which left the others. Steve . . . you did talk to Steve a lot. And he's a family man. Maybe you weren't seeing him at all. You could have spoken to him about wanting to find family. It could have been quite natural when you were talking about his kids for you to bring that up.

Same with Mr Cadwallader. Did you ask him for fatherly advice? Did he get too interested in you and take it the wrong way? Of everyone on the list, he seems to fit that charming, calculating side of the profile that Coombs told us about. Or am I now seeing smoke everywhere where there's no fire?

Obviously Oliver is a kind of freaky obsessive, but the police already checked him out. Did they check him well enough?

Aubrey had an alibi for when you went missing. Which doesn't entirely rule him out because you could have been meeting him later after he got off his shift. Which brings me back to wondering how many possibles are there that I don't even know of?

I really wish I could speak to Harry right now.

Dad said earlier that Harry can come over to say goodbye before we leave. Lying here in the dark, it's the first time I really think of how that's going to be. I know, Jenny, I said right from the start that loving him is going to prove to be my dumbest move ever. Soon, very soon, I'm going to have to say goodbye to him for the very last time. And after that I will never see him again.

I didn't think I had tears left in me to cry, but now I realise the inevitability of losing him, they soak the pillow.

CHAPTER 42

I wake heavy-eyed to a dull morning. Someone's knocking on my door – Dad probably – but I turn over and pull the quilt over my head. After five minutes of ignoring it, the room phone rings. I answer it simply to shut it up and of course it's Dad.

'Hannah, open the door. I need to speak to you. It's nearly ten.'

I let out a groan.

'Come down for breakfast. They finish serving in half an hour.'

'Do I get my phone back?'

'If you're here in time for breakfast, yes.'

I shuffle out of bed and shower in about two minutes,

cleaning my teeth at the same time. Five minutes later, I'm walking down to the lobby, pulling a comb through my wet hair. He meets me at the top of the stairs.

We plough our way through breakfast, glowering at each other.

'So what did the police say last night?' I ask finally, not to break the silence, but because it actually does matter a lot.

'Coombs will be over to speak to you himself soon but he said this: you need to be very careful. They went over to the hotel last night and interviewed everyone there again to see if anything new could be garnered, but Coombs wasn't optimistic about that at this stage. They think the killer might try to entice you into a trap so you must not make any response to him. They are considering whether seizing the phone and making some responses themselves might mean they can draw him in to their own trap, but their profiler is working on whether that's a good strategy.'

Coombs arrives about half an hour later and lays it on the line that I need to stop taking risks. Dad told him about my trip to Harry's and he's furious. But he agrees Harry is now no longer a suspect, which means Dad will let me see him. I suppose that's something positive.

As soon as Coombs is gone I get my phone back and text Harry. Can he possibly come over here this afternoon because I'm in lockdown?

He answers quickly. Yes, he'll bail out of the display this afternoon and be over after lunch.

It's a relief. There's only so long I can spend in my room reading about psychopaths before I lose it. At least now I have something to look forward to. Dad's doing some work, to keep his mind occupied. Lucky him – I wish I had something to do. We packed in such a rush I didn't bring any books with me and I haven't seen a bookstore. In fact, I haven't seen many stores at all.

Dad and I spend lunch silently glowering at each other again until I announce, 'Harry's coming over soon. We'll hang out upstairs seeing as how I'm locked in.'

Dad purses his lips and nods. 'Don't leave the hotel!' And then he relents and softens. 'I like that young man.'

'You do?' Wasn't particularly expecting that right now, I have to say.

'Yes. He's not glib. A boy shouldn't be glib if he's going out with my daughter, dammit. He should be terrified he's going to say or do the wrong things and lose her. Nervous is good. Nervous says he cares. Glib spells trouble.'

'Oh!' I digest this.

Dad eyes me with the ghost of a smile. 'I was a teenage boy once, you know.'

He waits for Harry in the lobby, to tell him I'm to stay in the hotel.

'Absolutely. She's not going anywhere,' Harry replies.

Great, my boyfriend is siding with my dad. This could only happen to me. I get back at Dad for the grounding by kissing the hell out of Harry for at least half an hour when I get him to my room. Most of it lying on the bed, for extra revenge.

'Wow,' says Harry when we finally stop to breathe for a while. 'What was that for?'

'To make up for last night,' I say.

He props himself on his elbow and looks at me. 'There was something I wanted to ask you about that.'

I'm not sure I want to drag it all up again, but I guess it's only fair that he gets to ask. 'OK.'

'You said there were three things that made you doubt me. The first two you told me, but you never mentioned the third.'

I rake through my memory. 'Oh yeah. OK, if you really want to know, it was the first day I met you. You looked at me like there was something you knew, but you weren't telling me. It made me suspicious at the time that you knew something about where Jenny had gone maybe. And then, once I knew she was dead, it made me wonder whether you were hiding something.'

He rolls on to his back, perplexed, and thinks. Then he lets out a shout of laughter. It makes me jump almost clean off the bed.

'What? What is it?'

He's curled up in a ball shaking with laughter. He can't speak.

I poke him. 'Tell me!'

He shakes his head, still curled up. I start to giggle too, just because it's funny to watch someone laugh so much, especially when you've caused it and have no idea why. Maybe I'm a little bit nervous too about what his answer's going to be.

'That's so funny,' he says eventually. 'I know what you mean. That is, I know exactly what it was I was thinking at the time that I didn't want you to know.'

'Well, tell me! The suspense is killing me.'

He leans back up on to his elbow and looks at me very seriously. 'I was thinking that you were beautiful, much more than your sister because you have more character in your face. And I was thinking that I had never come across a girl who completely blew me away the way you did just with a look and a few words, just by being herself so completely. And I was thinking I couldn't let you see that at all because I would . . .' He shrugs with his free shoulder. 'You know.'

Yes, I did know. If I had been him thinking that, I'd have died of shame if I thought he could read my feelings. This is why we work so well together.

I strike myself on the head. 'So you are telling me that I got all suspicious you knew something about Jenny, when actually you just thought I was hot?'

He grins. 'Yeah.'

I hold it together for a second and then I roll into him,

laughing as much as he was, and that sets him off again.

'It is just too, too dumb,' I gasp. I flop back on the bed and a moment later his hand takes mine and we lie together, staring at the ceiling, while we recover.

I hope you don't mind the laughing, Jenny. I think we both needed it.

'So I was hoping you could help me out with my suspect list,' I tell him. I get the pad out of my drawer and show him. I've torn off the part with his name on it. 'It's just there are so many people at Wolfscott and these are the only ones I know.'

He scans down the list. 'Yeah, that seems comprehensive.'

'Yes, too comprehensive. I can't narrow it down.'

'Steve, hmm. I don't think he fits the psychopath profile. Not from what you told me. He really doesn't like the hotel girls coming on to him. Also what you said about the animal cruelty. Absolutely no way. He'd be more likely to lynch someone for hurting an animal than to do it himself.'

'OK, that's useful.'

'Mr Cadwallader . . . interesting. I wouldn't have said so, but that's the point, I suppose. It's difficult to spot. He's a workaholic though so I don't know if your theory holds up. We know Jenny left site every afternoon and he was definitely always working then. But it's not impossible. Who else have you got? Oliver. Got to be honest, he seems more likely. The staff seem to think he's generally a bit weird. Doesn't exactly fit the profile of charming though. More creepy, and he did have a thing about Jenny. Michael I don't know at all. I had no idea until you told me that she was looking for her family. I see what you mean about the texts though. Surely it's too obvious that he would be a suspect?'

'I can't be certain but, yeah.'

'No, I think you're right. Let's see, Aubrey. I talk to him sometimes. He comes out the back of the kitchen to smoke when we're training the birds. I suppose everyone knows he's been inside. Personally, I think stealing a car when you're our age, which is what he did, isn't exactly a big indicator of being a murderer later.'

'Except that psychopaths do have a history of criminal behaviour and taking risks. It's part of the profile.'

'OK. Who else? . . . Oh . . . Tom.'

'Don't get offended. Remember I was putting everyone down.'

'Yeah, I was the bit at the bottom that got ripped off then.' He winks at me. 'Same again, isn't it? He wouldn't have talked to you so openly about her tracing family and then sent those texts. Although I didn't realise he knew her that well. Of course, I hardly speak to him so why would I?' He reads through my notes again. 'I'm not helping much. I need to think it over. Maybe something will come to me.'

'Thanks for trying anyway.'

He shakes his head. 'I mean it – I do need to think about it. I'm not a quick thinker. Always got told I was too slow at doing stuff in school, but when I can do it, I do it properly so I don't reckon speed is that important.'

I grin. 'It's not my way, but it makes sense to me.'

'There's something else I need to talk to you about,' he says rolling over on to his stomach. 'You're going back home soon, aren't you?'

I have that feeling like I'm going over the top of a rollercoaster, that part just before the descent and the elation, where instead your stomach hangs and is about to drop away, and it feels like dread. 'I guess. Dad wants us to go home as soon as Jenny's body is released by the pathologist. We need to take her home to Mom and Brandon.'

He reaches for my hands, his face turned towards me. 'I always knew we were on borrowed time. But I wanted to talk to you about what happens next.'

I swallow.

'I don't want it to be over when you leave.'

Looking at him now, I can't imagine getting on a plane and never seeing his face again. Never feeling his lips kiss mine. It's unthinkable.

'So I was thinking, I need a plan.'

I nod. I shouldn't. I should tell him that these things never work and we must face up to it. But I can't force those words out because I don't want to hear them.

'I'm eighteen in a few months. If it's what you want too, I'll look into getting a visa to come over to the US. To work, I mean. I did some reading up and I could get the same kind of work over there as I do here. It just has to be all sorted before I can get a visa so it'll take some planning.' He holds my hands to his lips. 'But I have to know if it's what you want too.'

That first time he kissed me, what was it I thought?

. . . the most lunatic insanity in my head — that now and forever this is where I want to be, who I want to be and who I want to be with.

And all at once, from nowhere and for no reason I can explain even to myself, I am in love.

I've known all along that I don't want to let him go. I've just been telling myself it's unavoidable.

If I don't try and I let him go, it'll butcher my heart, and if I try to keep him and he drifts away, my heart will be torn apart too. I know what you would say, Jenny. You'd tell me I may as well try then.

I guess you'd be right. What is there to lose? I can fight and fail, or I can not fight and lose anyway. And maybe, just maybe, I'll fight and win.

I squeeze his hand hard. 'Yes, it's what I want.'

He kisses me. He kisses me like we're running out of time.

CHAPTER 43

At seven the next morning I am woken by a new text arriving. This one's a real surprise.

Hi Hannah, it's Tom. Can you meet me at 9? I think I've remembered something vital, but I don't want to give the game away so I have to be careful who sees me. Meet me by the back gate ☺

My heart pounds. Could this finally be a real breakthrough? It's five miles back to Wolfscott. If I set out now, I can walk it. And I need to leave before Dad comes to check on me. It sounds like Tom is taking a risk so I can't let him down.

I text a yes back to him and then shower at warp speed, throwing my hair up into a messy bun rather than have the hassle of washing and drying it. I check the lobby – no one out there – and then I make my escape down the stairs. I sneak past the dining room, then I'm outside, jogging down the drive before Dad realises I'm gone.

I get to the back gate just before nine. It's an arched wooden gate with a thumb latch. I open it carefully and peek inside. It leads on to a path that skirts round the woodland at Wolfscott and is the quickest way up to the old lookout point on Wolf Cliff. There's no one around so I go through and close the gate. As I turn round, Tom appears at my shoulder.

'Oh! You made me jump!'

He puts his hand on my arm in apology. 'Sorry! I was trying to keep out of sight. Wait a sec.' He hurries over to an oak tree and returns with a shotgun, broken over his arm. 'Needed an excuse to be out here in case I was seen, so this is it – bagging a few rabbits,' he says.

Seeing the gun shouldn't freak me out so much, but somehow it does. 'I didn't know you owned one.'

'No reason you should. I use it on the big pheasant shoots here in autumn and winter.'

All right, that explains it. You mentioned that once when we were Skyping. I remember how your face screwed up in distaste because you don't like hunting. 'So what have you found out?'

'Sshh, not here,' he hisses, looking around. 'Let's take a walk and I'll explain my theory.'

I was hoping for something more solid than a theory, but I guess I'll hear him out.

We weave up the path for a way in silence, before Tom turns upwards on to a narrower track.

I can't wait any longer. 'So tell me, what's your theory.'

He pushes his hand through his hair. 'I need to backtrack a little. You know I told you Jenny was working on tracing her family?'

'Yeah.'

'I didn't quite tell you all of it.'

'What?' I stop and glare at him. Actually, I want to hit him.

He holds his hands up in a placatory gesture. 'Hey, I said to you from the outset I was working on the assumption that she was fine. I had reasons for not telling you more right then.'

I let my breath out long and slow in an attempt to diffuse my anger. 'What reasons?'

He casts another look around. 'Jenny started off researching your mother. She was looking for aunts, uncles, cousins, with the aim of creating a family tree. She called your mother and asked her what her maiden name was, but your mother wouldn't tell her.'

None of this is news to me, except Mom hadn't exactly told me that last part.

'Your mother told her in no uncertain terms to back off and stop looking or she'd have your dad come and take her home.'

OK, Mom definitely didn't tell me that and I'm betting Dad didn't know either. Why did Mom lie about it?

Or had you lied to Tom?

'Jenny was really quite angry about that. So she tried another route, researching deaths in boating accidents because that's how your mother said her parents died. And that's how Jenny found out her maiden name was Winstanley.'

I breathe in sharply. Serena Winstanley – our mother. I can see how you would have treasured that knowledge.

'So she had the start of her family tree. As your mother said she was an only child, Jenny then began looking to see if her grandparents had brothers and sisters.'

I glance up the path which continues upwards even more steeply. 'OK. Where are we going, by the way?'

'Up to Wolf Cliff. It's usually quiet up there. We can talk properly.'

I pick my way past a difficult patch with a steep gradient and tree roots waiting to trip me up. 'What has this got to do with who killed her though?'

'I'm getting to that,' Tom says, giving me a hand to pull me up. 'Nearly there. So what happened next is that Jenny traced a relative.'

'Really?'

'Really. And she met up with him.'

I stop talking to negotiate the last part of the track and then we come on to the summit of Wolf Cliff. It's a high point that looks over the fields below. There's a sheer drop from the edge where a landslide eroded the sandstone rock centuries before – that's in the hotel blurb Wolfscott give out too. I catch my breath and then look expectantly at him.

He smiles. 'You're sure you want to hear this?'

Can he doubt it? 'If it helps catch the man who killed my sister, yes!'

'Don't you want to hear it for yourself? It is your family too.'

I contemplate the point. 'Not really. I'm going home as soon as Jenny's body is released and we can take her back with us. I've had it with England.'

He looks out across the fields. 'What would it take, I wonder, to get your mother to come over here?'

'Huh?' I'm about to ask him what the hell he's talking about when my phone vibrates. A text from Harry.

Where are you? I need to see you NOW.

I start to text a reply when there's a sharp pain in my head and everything goes black.

CHAPTER 44

My eyes feel like they're glued together. My head feels as if someone buried an axe in it. I attempt to reach up, but I can't move my arms. When I open my eyes, sending a dart of pain through my skull, I find I'm sitting with my back against a tree and my hands tied firmly behind me. My ankles are tied too.

Tom is pointing the shotgun directly at me. 'It's loaded,' he says pleasantly.

'So it was you.' Speaking hurts.

'Yes.' He smiles. It's a charming smile of English pretty-boy perfection.

'Why?'

He laughs, throwing his head back. 'Oh, I was so hoping you were going to ask that.'

He leans against a tree. A glance around shows me we're only a few metres from the cliff edge. It's obvious why he wanted to bring me up here, away from everybody. Will he shoot me? Will he strangle me? Or will he just throw me over the edge and let the sandstone boulders do the job for him?

'Let me tell you a story. It's a true story. Once upon a time, there was a young boy who lived with his mother and father. His mother was much younger than his father. She was an orphan and perhaps she was looking for a father figure when she married the older man, who was a vicar. He was certainly a stern individual.' He pauses. 'Don't you think I'm telling this well? I quite like the effect. No? Never mind, I'll go on anyway. It's not like you're going anywhere.' He laughs again.

'So the little boy grows up in a house where only his mother shows him any affection at all. Until the day she leaves. She just ups and goes. No goodbyes, nothing. He is five years old. When he's brave enough to ask his father where she went, after days and nights of expecting her to come back to him, his father tells him that she's run off to America with another man. A man she met while he was over here on a business trip.'

I am ice all over.

'I told your sister this story,' he says. 'She looked much the same as you do now.'

I try to speak, but nothing will come out and I don't know what I'm trying to say anyway.

'So the boy grows up in the house alone with his father. She divorced him, you see, from overseas, so she was free to marry her businessman. Then his father marries again, and he and his new wife have another child – a boy. But still nobody has any time for our hero.'

He isn't even being sarcastic. That more than anything makes my heart pound with fear.

'The stepmother dies some years later, of cancer. And the vicar takes up a new job in the parish where a large estate is situated. He continues to be a cold, unloving father, seeming to favour our hero least, although he can't be said to show affection to either child.'

A noise on the track stops his story mid-flow and I see Harry burst into the clearing, with Merlin on his arm. I try to scream out a warning, but it's too late. The sound of birdsong is halted by the crack of a shotgun firing. Harry's body hits the ground and the hawk flies for the trees.

I scream again. Harry's holding his leg and his face is knotted with pain. But he's still alive.

'Don't move,' Tom says. 'There's still another cartridge.'

'You always were a crap shot,' Harry grinds out through his teeth, gripping his thigh to staunch the blood.

A flash of anger crosses Tom's face and I know Harry hit his mark. 'Maybe I'm not done with you yet,' Tom says. 'I could use you showing up here like her knight in shining armour to my advantage. Er, a word of advice though, little half-brother – if you want to play knight, you're supposed to win, not get yourself shot down.' Tom swings the barrel of the gun back at me. 'It's good you arrived now though, in time for the rest of the story.'

Harry looks right at me. His eyes are trying to communicate something, but I don't understand what.

'As our hero grows older, he gets a little fire into his blood, the way boys can, and one day after a fight with the old man, he decides he'd be better off without him so he waits until his brother is out and then he torches the house with the old man in it. He covers his tracks well though. The authorities are not suspicious of arson and the conclusion is that the old man had so much junk lying around the place that the fire, which started from a spark from the grate on to the carpet, took an unstoppable hold.'

'You killed Dad?' Harry's face is as white as a sheet.

'Don't pretend you loved him. He meant as little to you as he did to me.'

'He was still my dad.'

Tom's eyes are utterly uncomprehending and I start to understand exactly what all those descriptions of psychopathic traits really mean. 'Stupid sentimentality. That's why you'll never be anything in life.'

'Because becoming a murderer is such a good career move.'

It's a dumb thing to say, but I can't help it.

He gives me an amused look. 'It's not so bad when you don't get caught. Which is where little half-brother here comes in.'

'So you told Jenny all this?'

'I haven't quite finished my story yet. The estate that the vicar lived on felt sorry for the orphans and offered them work and housing in return for their father's years of service. Our hero took on the guardianship of his half-brother and they got on with their lives. Until one day a girl walked into the place where our hero worked.'

Oh God, oh God, oh God.

'She was American and the absolute image of our hero's mother. Same eyes, same hair, same curves to her face. It was like looking at his mother returned to him and frozen in time. He had to know how this came to be, so he befriended her and she gave away all her secrets, silly girl. Even her mother's name. Of course, once our hero knew her story, he knew who she was. Knew she was his half-sister.'

There's a horrified gasp from Harry who missed the beginning. I can see blood pooling on the ground beneath him. If he doesn't get help soon, he's going to bleed to death.

'So he encouraged her to start trying to trace her family. And he pointed her in the direction of someone who could help her. But she gave up too soon. He had to carry on with the rest of his plan for revenge though, so he would just have to convince her of what her mother had done himself – how she'd abandoned her son for some man she hardly knew, ran a whole continent away and left her child with a father who couldn't love him. How she let that son grow up motherless, wondering if she'd ever come back, hoping against hope that she would. That she'd remember him and that she at least would love him. But that never happened. So he arranged to meet his half-sister when she went off for a walk.' He laughs. 'I believe you know the rest.'

'But why did you kill her? Why?'

He waves a dismissive hand at me. 'It makes perfect sense. I killed her to be the flame to draw the moth in.'

'What the hell are you taking about, you maniac?'

'I thought if I killed her, her mother . . . *my* mother . . . would come here,' he explains as if he's talking to a three-year-old. 'Would come to find her daughter. What mother wouldn't?'

'But she couldn't come because Brandon was sick . . .' His twisted thinking is starting to make monstrous sense.

'That has been an inconvenience.' He walks over to Harry, pointing the gun at his head, and I wriggle frantically, trying to loosen the ropes even though I know it's hopeless.

He kicks Harry hard on his injured leg and then watches, smiling, as he writhes on the ground in agony.

'Brothers,' he says, turning back to me. 'Such a nuisance.' His eyes are glittering with excitement – there's no humanity in them at all. 'It was going to be payback time. Twice. One, she loses a daughter. Two, she shows up here and she dies. After her other daughter dies in front of her eyes, of course.'

'You were going to kill me and my mom?'

'Oh yes. That was the whole point of bringing you here. I thought watching you die first was a nice touch. I couldn't do that with Jenny because she was only the lure. I had some fun with that though. It was quite a delicate operation – took a lot of my skills to pull it all off. First I had to convince Jenny she needed to seriously look for her family. Then that she needed to squirrel away some money out of sight to help her trace them. She might need to make some visits, pay for taxis, hotel stays, that kind of thing. She bought it, but getting Cassie to lend her the documents to open an account was tough!' He grins. 'Cassie was suspicious I was interested in Jenny, and Cassie always had a thing about me so she didn't like that idea. But I managed to play her well enough to convince her she was just helping out a friend. It didn't go quite to plan in the end: Jenny was supposed to go to the train station that last day and book a ticket to our mother's old family home. I was to tell the Cadwalladers she'd been called away for a few days and make her apologies. But she got suspicious too soon so I had to move into the next stage of the plan – killing her. Still, it all left a nice little red herring to keep the police busy. And when you started snooping around, talking to Cassie, it was obvious she'd give the game away sooner or later, so that made my mind up for me – she had to go too.'

'What the hell kind of monster are you?'

He bends down and looks me right in the face. 'Who is the monster here? Me, or the woman who created me and then abandoned me? Your mother made me what I am. She left me here with a father who had no love for me, while she got to live her happy family dream in the US. Don't pull your sanctimonious little face at me. You would kill me yourself now if you could. You're no different to me – we have half the same genes. In another life, you could *be* me.'

'I could never be you,' I spit back at him. 'My mom didn't make you like this. You're just pure evil.'

'If she had abandoned you, if you had been through what I have, if you had had my life . . . in my life, you would be me,' he snarls. 'Don't kid yourself you'd be any different.'

'Don't kid yourself I wouldn't!'

He straightens up. 'You're boring me now. Time to die.' He throws the gun down on the grass and grabs me under the armpits. As he drags me towards the edge of the cliff, I cast a desperate look at Harry who is trying, white-lipped, to struggle on to one knee.

I can thrash about, but I can't fight him. I'm too trussed up. 'What are you going to do with Harry?' I ask, playing for time even though it's pointless.

'Harry's body will be found next to yours, with his head blown off. And there'll be some texts on your phones that will help explain it all to the police. You found out he was the killer so he killed you. And then killed himself.'

I can see the ghastly logic.

'I win,' he says as pleasantly as if he's discussing what to have for dinner. 'I walk away from this without suspicion. And surely your mother can't ignore the fact she's lost two daughters. She'll have to come over now. A distraught parent killing herself – that wouldn't seem unrealistic. My plans may have altered a little, but I'll still achieve the same aim.'

'She won't come. She still has Brandon to take care of. And Dad's here to take my body home, so she won't come – he won't let her. But you hate her so much that you'd kill her? Your own mother?'

'She had no right to leave me. She deserves what she gets. If she doesn't come then no, I don't get to finish it as I wanted but she gets to suffer for the rest of her life because she's lost all her children. If you want someone to blame for your sister's death, if you want someone to blame in your last moments as you fall towards your own death, then blame your mother. Our mother.'

I'm limp with hopelessness and horror at what he is as he drags me further towards the cliff edge. He's chuckling softly.

And then, just at the very limits of my hearing, I hear the

quietest of whistles. From my peripheral vision, I see a hawk swoop out of the trees.

Merlin lands on his master's wrist. Harry whispers to the bird and shifts his gaze to mine. Then slowly and deliberately as Tom reaches the cliff edge and begins to drag my torso over, Harry raises his hand.

The hawk flies.

There, in that familiar targeted flight low across the ground, like a bullet, Merlin flies straight to me. Tom's skewed round. He doesn't see the bird coming.

I stretch my head to the side and raise my right shoulder – my arm is trussed up, but Merlin understands. He lands there as Tom turns his face back towards me.

I jerk my shoulder up as hard I can to give the bird his cue. Tom's eyes widen for a brief second as he sees a flurry of feathers and talons flying into his face. He reels back and his foot catches on the edge of the cliff as he tries to tear the bird off him. For a moment, he hangs there, suspended against the sky. Then topples back over the edge and falls with a scream that echoes down, down, down.

Harry drags himself over to me as fast as he can, scrambling across the grass. As he reaches me, the hawk circles back above the cliff again, soaring and swooping in what looks like a triumphant dance. Predator on predator. Only one winner.

Harry flops on to his back, holding his arm up, panting in relief. 'I thought you were gone too, stupid,' he says to the hawk as it settles on his wrist again. 'You weren't supposed to go over with him, you doofus!'

I lie on the cliff edge and look down at the body spreadeagled below on the rocks. It doesn't move.

That was almost me.

A hawk. That was what saved me. Saved us. Without Merlin, we'd be nothing but Tom's trophies.

That thing lying smashed below us is my half-brother. It feels like no matter how much I shower I will never be clean again.

I begin to shiver uncontrollably.

CHAPTER 45

It was Harry who called the cops. I was all but useless, but I kept pressure on his injured leg with both my hands until they came. His blood oozed between my fingers as I lay beside him, terrified he would die. I could feel him growing colder from the blood loss.

He wouldn't get into the ambulance until he knew Merlin was safe so I used his phone to call Steve while the paramedics worked on his leg. The falconer was red and sweating when he arrived, bursting through the treeline much as Harry had done earlier.

'I've never run so fast in my life,' Steve said, leaning over with his hands on his knees and panting to get his breath back. 'Is he going to be OK?'

'He should be,' the paramedic replied, 'but we need to move him now. We couldn't have waited much longer. Her too – that head wound needs attention.'

I was wrapped in a space blanket, still shaking. I don't even remember being put into the ambulance.

All the way to the hospital in the ambulance, and even now, I can't stop reliving those moments on the cliff. They play over and over in my head, like a film on a loop.

Maybe, Jenny, there will always now be a part of me up there waiting to fall. I cheated death. You didn't. How is that justice? How will I live with this? That you died and I didn't. Tom is dead, but the damage he has done continues. There are wounds that will fester and never heal. There is guilt. So much guilt I think I'll never bear it.

The paramedic speaks to me. I can't respond. I can't even hear her – there are words, but my brain refuses to process what her words are and what they mean.

I'm still on the cliff.

I'm the next victim.

Harry will be after me.

I don't remember being taken to a hospital cubicle. I don't remember a doctor. I have a vague awareness of people looking and talking, but that's all it is – an impression. It's only when Dad arrives, flinging back the curtain, his face white and terrorised, that I come to and find myself in a hospital bed in the emergency department.

'Hannah,' he says. No more than that, just my name.

I wake up from the nightmare and I hold my arms out to him, as you and I used to do when we were little girls waking from bad dreams. Dad holds me. He's wearing that same aftershave he always wears, the one Mom buys him. This is the smell of my father. This is the man who has changed my diapers, told me countless times that everything will be all right as he's dried my tears, bandaged cut knees, picked me up from school. The man who has loved me every day of my life. If anyone can pull me back from hell, he can.

Does he know? Does he know about Mom? I have to ask.

'The guy who did it, he said he was Mom's son,' I mumble into his shoulder as he holds me tight. 'Did you know she had a kid here, before us?'

Dad sits back, enough shock etched on his face, replacing the shadows of fear and trauma that lingered there, that I know he knew nothing of Tom or Mom's life here. Not the life Tom described anyway.

'What are you talking about?' he asks in confusion, searching my face as if he suspects I'm babbling from the head injury.

'What did the cops tell you?'

'That you and your boyfriend had both been injured in a struggle with another young man, who they now believe to be

266

the person who killed Jenny. That he died and that you were brought here, along with your boyfriend who's been shot.'

I lean my forehead on his arm. 'I guess that's it, more or less.'

'What did you mean about Mom?'

'The guy, Tom. He killed Jenny, and Cassie. He said he was Mom's son from her first marriage.'

'What first marriage?'

I lift my head and look at Dad, hearing his tone of incredulity. But I see it there – that tiny flicker of uncertainty in his eyes. And I know Tom's telling the truth. Dad's doubt tells me all I need to know.

'I think I need to talk to Mom,' I tell him.

'You need to rest first,' he says firmly, laying me back against the pillows. 'Your head is hurt and they want to keep you here for a few hours for monitoring. Then you know you'll have to be interviewed by the police.'

'Not until tomorrow, Dad, please. Ask them to wait.'

'I'll try, honey.' Then he just holds me and I hold him back without words. It's the only way to be when there's nothing in the universe that can make things better.

Coombs drops by while they make me rest. He nods at me, his lips compressed. 'I need you to confirm for me that the version of events I've been given is correct. Tom was the one responsible for your sister's death and the attack on you?'

'Yes,' I reply, sounding as weak as I feel.

'That's all I need for now. The young lad can tell me the rest. I'll come back when you're better.' And he disappears, presumably to talk to Harry.

I close my eyes and wonder painfully if I should have let him go. Harry probably doesn't feel up to talking to him either. But I'm too tired, too bone-weary to argue with myself any longer. When the doctor suggests a shot to help me sleep, I don't argue. Getting away from all of this is a relief.

CHAPTER 46

It's Harry who wakes me. He's sitting beside the bed with his leg in bandages and my hand is held tightly in his.

'I thought you were never going to wake up.'

I open my mouth to speak, but my lips are dry and only a croak comes out. He passes me some water from a cupboard beside the bed. It tastes warm and stale, but I drink it down. 'Have you been here long?' I finally manage to get out.

'About an hour. They fixed my leg up, then I needed blood.' He shrugs as if it's nothing. 'Then the police wanted to speak to me.'

'I'm sorry.'

He squeezes my hand gently. 'How are you feeling?'

'I-I-I don't know, to be truthful.'

His beautiful, clear, understanding eyes look into mine. 'What you need to understand is that none of this is your fault. Or anyone but Tom's. I keep beating myself up for not having realised earlier that it was him. I should have, you know.'

'Why? How could you have known?'

He sighs. 'Because, you know, I'm . . . I was . . . his brother. There's stuff about him . . . I should just have seen him for what he was.'

'Like what?'

He hangs his head, not in shame I think, but because it's hard to talk about. 'Remember how I told you we never had pets when I was a kid? I never had a single one until I moved out into the cottage and got Merlin. That's because he was shitty to me when I was a kid and I had this fear if I had a pet that –' He stops and bites his lip.

'That something bad would happen to it?'

'Yeah, I guess.'

'So when I mentioned the animal cruelty –'

'But that's just it, Hannah. I never saw him be cruel to an animal. I didn't think he'd be cruel to my pet, if I had one, because he wanted to hurt an animal.'

I shake my head. 'Sorry, I don't understand then.'

'It was me he'd be getting back at. He'd hurt it to get at me.' Harry shuffles his feet and probes a deep scratch on his hand with a cautious finger. 'I thought it was just the way it is with some brothers. We sort of hated each other. He was the older one and made my life hard because of that.'

Reading his face in growing anger, I translate 'hard' as 'hell'. 'So he took out his anger with your dad and, well, with my mom, I guess, on you.' I would never be able to bring myself to say 'our mom'.

Harry sighs heavily. 'Anyway, that's how I eventually guessed. I thought about how he was when we were kids and what you told me and it suddenly made sense. Mostly these days I avoided him, and everyone else seemed to like him.' He shakes his head sadly at me. 'I just thought he'd grown out of being a shit, when actually what happened is he grew into a worse one.'

'Did you know all the stuff about his mom?' I still can't put his mom and my mom together in my head.

'My mum told me she left when Tom was little and that's all I knew. Didn't know she'd gone to America. Dad never mentioned her and Tom didn't either.'

'I'm sorry about your dad.'

His face hardens. 'You know, he was a long way from being the greatest dad in the world, but he was a million miles from being the worst. How could Tom do that?' His face is twisted with hate for his brother, but his eyes are full of bewilderment. 'He's just evil, Hannah. It's the only explanation.'

I want to agree with him, but some part of me is scared by

271

what Tom said. Did Mom do this to him by leaving? Did she warp that little boy into a monster?

CHAPTER 47

I'm fit to be discharged on the following day. They kept me in overnight as a precaution. Dad whispered it was because they didn't want the police bugging me until I'd had a night's sleep. I leave with some painkillers and an information sheet about head injury so we knew the signs to watch out for in case there was a problem.

To my surprise, Mr Cadwallader turns up in his BMW to collect Harry. He and Dad met in the parking lot and he comes in to see me before he gets Harry from the ward.

I am embarrassed to see him, given he was at one point my number-one suspect.

'Hannah, I am so dreadfully sorry,' he says.

'You couldn't have known. Even Harry didn't guess until

the end,' I reply, trying to stop blushing.

'He seemed such a polite young man.' Mr Cadwallader shrugs helplessly. 'And he'd had quite a tragic early life. To come out of that appearing so well-adjusted and charming. He was great with the customers . . . I didn't suspect a thing.'

But that's the point, isn't it? Tom played all of us beautifully. I think I'm beginning to understand that was all part of the 'game' for him. The more he lied and got away with, the bigger the win.

I feel dirty and wrong for knowing that, for understanding him at that level.

In another life, you could be me.

I shudder and refocus so I can stop thinking about him.

'What will happen to Harry now?'

Mr Cadwallader smiles in relief at being able to give some good news. I guess he doesn't want to talk about Tom either. It must be creepy to know you sheltered *that* under your roof for all that time. 'Harry will come back with me. We want him to stay in the castle until his leg has healed up. And Steve says he'll want a room with a view of the birds, so I can certainly arrange that.'

'He'll keep his job and his cottage?'

'Of course!' He appears shocked I ask. 'Harry is an excellent employee and he's been through a horrendous experience. He'll have our support for as long as he needs it.'

Maybe that's the answer with Mr Cadwallader. Maybe that's why he blows hot and cold with his staff. A simple thing like he's hard on them until they really need his help and then he'll do anything for them. I kind of get that, and I feel my cheeks grow hot with renewed embarrassment that I thought he could be a cold-blooded murderer. At least he doesn't know and that's my saving grace. I smile as best I can. 'That's good to know.'

He turns to Dad. 'I expect you'll be going home soon.'

'A matter of days now. Look, I'm sorry for my rudeness when we left. We really are very grateful for your hospitality.'

They exchange some polite words and then Mr Cadwallader goes to find Harry. I'm going back to the hotel to change and shower properly and then I'm expected at the police station to make my statement.

I wave goodbye to Harry as he leaves and try not to think how soon I'll be waving goodbye for the last time.

I said the last time I was in this police station that I only wanted to be here again if your killer had been caught. I guess I got my wish, though I didn't quite plan it this way. Taking my statement is no big deal after everything else that's happened and Coombs makes sure he's involved which makes it easier on me.

When it's all over, Dad needs to take a call to arrange our journey back with . . . you. Coombs leans back in his chair when Dad goes out and says, 'You shouldn't pay attention to anything Tom said, you know.'

'Why not?'

'Because that's his *modus operandi* – to play with you. And that's what he was doing.'

'It doesn't make what he said a lie though. Not automatically. What if what he became is as a result of what happened to him?'

'Well, that's the million-dollar question we'd all love to solve. The psychologists especially.'

'What do you think?'

He puts his hands behind his head and stretches his legs out. 'I think people like him aren't like the rest of us. Most people couldn't become like him because there's always something inside that would stop them. The psychopath lacks that.'

'But not all psychopaths kill.'

'No and that's where it gets interesting. Can he blame what happened to him for his slide into killing innocent people?' He purses his lips and shakes his head. 'I don't think we'll ever know. Certainly asking the Toms of this world won't give us an answer. The psychopath blames others for his actions – that's part of his character too. It'll never be his fault.'

I digest this, seeing the truth of it, but still questioning whether there's more to it.

'Hannah, all over the world, every day, people have far worse things happen to them than Tom did. But they don't go and do what he did. We have to be accountable for our actions.'

That's true too. But there's still that question. If Mom hadn't left, if Tom had had her there while he grew up, would he ever have killed?

And I still don't know the answer to that. I never will.

CHAPTER 48

I get a call from Harry to say he's back in his cottage. Didn't like all the fuss, he texted, and he was fine anyway. Could I come round?

I have to. I was about to text him anyway.

We're going home tomorrow, Jenny. All of us. The pathologist has released you and it's time to go back. Mom and Brandon are waiting for you.

I haven't talked to Mom about Tom yet. I guess Dad must have but I haven't asked him. It still makes me feel sick to think I'm related to *that*.

What all this means though, Jenny, is that I get Dad to drive me over to Harry's cottage and drop me off there. As we travel, I can see Strawlins Point above us from the road. I wonder if I should go up there again before we leave. But no, you're not there any more. It's not like I'm saying goodbye to you. You'll be with us. The police told me people have put flowers up there for you and Cassie, so perhaps I should go do the same.

'I'll text you when I'm ready,' I say to Dad as I get out of the car.

'That's OK,' he replies. I guess he knows I want my space to say goodbye.

Harry stands in the doorway, leaning against the frame. His weight rests on his uninjured leg.

'Hi,' he says, watching the car pull away.

As soon as it's out of sight, he bends his head and kisses me, long and slow. Neither of us are in a hurry to break away and I'm guessing he senses this will be our last time together.

When we do break apart, it's because he's shifting his weight and I realise he needs to sit down. I push him towards a chair.

'I'll make coffee,' I say. I don't actually want coffee, but it gives me something to do. I understand at this moment why Harry hates words. Maybe I'll try it his way. Maybe we'll do without them.

So I make the coffee and he watches me and neither of us speaks. And while it's this way, time isn't passing and my departure isn't getting closer and closer. There is me. There is him. That is all.

I sit on my knees in front of him, the way he sat in front of me when I was last here. He takes my face in his hands, cupping it gently as if I am a thing that can be easily broken.

'If I had known what he could do, and what he would do to you,' Harry says, so quietly that even in the silence of the cottage I have to lean closer to hear him, 'I would have stabbed him in his sleep to stop him.'

You could say, Jenny, and I suppose some people would, that Harry's is the wrong attitude to take. That I should feel wary of a boy who can say that and mean it, for he certainly does mean it.

But I understand feeling that way, Jenny. I understand better than anyone how that *thing* that hurt you can make a person feel like that. So I say nothing, but my eyes tell him it's OK.

'I don't want you to go,' he says softly, 'and I know that's what you've come here to tell me.'

I reach up and kiss him again. He tastes of instant coffee and loss.

His fingers trace the lines of my face. And when they've finished they begin doing so again. 'I want to memorise you,' he says, 'so I don't forget a single thing until I see you again.'

I have no courage now either for I lay my head in his lap and let him stroke my hair.

The time is coming when the clock must start ticking again, but I will hold on here for as long as I can.

After a while, he says, 'What is it, Hannah?'

And my heart fills with grief again. I lift my face and I know there are tears brimming in my eyes. 'We leave in the morning. Really early. I came to say goodbye.'

He nods. 'And?'

He knows there's more. Am I so transparent, or only to him?

'What you said, about coming to America – I don't want you to.'

He stills. And by that, Jenny, I mean he goes completely still. I'm not sure he's breathing as my words kill everything precious.

'He'll always be there between us. This will never leave me.' This next part is so hard to say that I feel as if I am literally dying as I speak the words. 'I am his blood. And you are his blood. That taints us. The stain of what he's done. It will never work, Harry, so it's better we say goodbye now.'

I expect him to be sad, or angry, or to get up and push me away. Instead he sits there so still and so quiet that I begin to wonder if somehow he hasn't even heard me.

'Harry?'

He smiles at me. It's the slightest of smiles, but there's a warmth shining out of his eyes that is unmistakable. It engulfs me.

'It'll change,' he says. 'We can make it change. He will not win. We can't let him.'

'No, I understand that he shouldn't, but –'

'No, Hannah. He won't.' His fingers caress the length of my hair. 'It's different for you. This is new and you're still in shock from it all. But I've lived with him all my life and he's made it miserable. Then you came along and it started to be amazing. I didn't know life could be like that. He is not taking that away. He's dead. He can only hurt us now if we let him.'

It's me who gets up and steps away, arms folded around myself.

'I know what you feel now,' he says and he doesn't follow me. 'But there will be a time when that changes. And when that day comes, you tell me and I will come. Will you promise me if that happens you'll tell me?'

I shake my head briskly, heading for the door before I weaken and cry, or weaken and tell him I don't want to leave him, ever. Because he's wrong. Tom has as much power dead as he did alive. I feel that power in how my stomach turns every time I think of him.

'Hannah, promise me!'

I'm at the door and about to run. There will be no last kiss, no lingering goodbyes. I can't bear it. I don't even look at him. 'If that ever should happen, I'll tell you,' I say over my shoulder in a flat voice. 'But it won't.'

And then I'm running, slamming the door behind me, out on to the path and away towards Wolfscott.

CHAPTER 49

The plane takes us home, Jenny. Dad sleeps, exhausted, great dark circles under his eyes like he hasn't slept for weeks. I cry silent tears into the blanket covering me. It's dawn outside and we're flying back into a future where you're only with us in memories and Harry is a memory to be forgotten.

I think my heart is beyond broken. It's simply destroyed.

Our reunion is as you'd expect: tears, hugging, the gratefulness of the living for each other, mixed with the desperation of grief for the missing one. Mom and Dad go upstairs to talk. No one wants Brandon to hear. I take him in to the yard to toss a baseball around while they talk and my stomach churns with nerves throughout.

It takes a while before he asks in a small, flat voice, 'Are you OK, Hannah?'

Unaccountably I have to swallow hard to answer, 'Yeah, I guess. Mostly. Better now I'm home.'

He rolls the ball around his glove, staring at it. 'I can't believe I'm never going to see her again. I thought it'd be me who didn't make it to being grown up, not Jenny.'

It's the small things that make us lose it, isn't it, Jenny? Brandon's little bewildered face, words voicing thoughts we'd never have wanted him to have . . . and suddenly there are hot tears on my cheeks and I can't breathe with the loss.

I sink to my knees on the grass. I feel his thin arms wrap around my neck and we hold on to each other. He cries too; I hear him in my ear. We understand each other in this grief for you.

It's a long, long time before Mom comes down and when she does she's pallid and shaking. Dad has hold of her hand and his face is bleached of colour too, but there's a set to his jaw that tells me he's holding her up through all of this.

I wonder if he and I will ever talk about what she did. Not yet, I guess, because neither of us is ready. As we look between each other's faces, there's a silence that is all about you.

It goes on until Dad breaks it. It had to be Dad because no one else knows how to.

'We're going to go make dinner together,' he says. 'All of

us. And then we're going to sit down and eat together. Then I'll make popcorn and we'll all watch a movie.'

For those who don't know us, that might seem callous. But not to us, because that's what we like doing as a family. That's what you loved doing – family time just hanging out together, popcorn, movie, sprawling out on the couches together.

It's Dad's way of bringing you home to us.

It's days before Mom and I talk about it. I can't find the words to bring you up . . . bring *him* up . . . and it seems like she can't either. In the end I think it's Dad who engineers it. He takes Brandon out somewhere and leaves us alone.

'Honey, we need to talk,' she says. 'About Jenny.'

So it's time. And there's only one place that feels right to do this, so I take her to the tree house. It's the only time she's ever been in there with me.

'I talked to Dad,' she says, drawing with her finger in the dust on the floor. It reminds me of you. 'I don't know how he's managed to forgive me, but he says he has. I'll never forgive myself.'

'I don't understand, Mom.' The words come very hard and I'm not sure they're the right ones. 'The police checked out what . . . what *he* said and . . .' I stare at her, not knowing how to go on.

'You want to know how I could do it,' she says and her

finger is shaking tracing in that dust. 'And how I could keep it all a secret, even from Dad.'

I nod, mute.

'Because I love you all so much and what we have here is so wonderful that I didn't want to ruin it. I never thought I'd have to, because that was another life, Hannah.'

An icy shiver runs up my spine.

'It's why I didn't want her to go. I didn't want any link to that life. But I never for one second imagined that she would come into contact with anyone I'd . . . left . . . over there. I would have dragged her home from the airport myself if I had.' Her eyes hold the same unshed tears mine do.

I nod again because I have no idea what to say to her. I want to be angry because that's what I do to get through but I can't find the fire within me to stoke a rage. Inside me, it's all cold and numb and lost.

'I owe you an explanation,' Mom says and a tear spills down her cheek, but she carries on. 'It's more than time. Dad told me what Tom said to you.'

Hearing his name on her lips is like a whiplash on my skin. I think it hurts her to say it too but it's more complex for her.

'I made a terrible mistake when I was younger, Hannah. I had no one after my parents died and when I met Tom's father, I was only Jenny's age.'

I clench my fists hearing your name next to his and Mom is

crying properly now, but she brushes the tears away and looks me in the eyes.

'He represented security and all the things I'd lost when I lost my parents. He said he loved me, and it was easier to be with him than alone so I told myself I loved him too. Stupidly I accepted when he proposed to me after a few months. It wasn't security with him at all – it was possession and I found that out quickly. He was a very controlling man, and a very jealous one.' She stops to compose herself for a second. 'We had a baby and I thought I'd have to make the best of it. I tried to – I really did for several years. And then something happened. I met your dad when he was over on business. We met in a coffee shop where we both . . . so silly . . . we both went for the last muffin. Our hands clashed and he let me take it, of course. I knew straight off, Hannah. We talked and it was wonderful and he was who I wanted to be with forever. I had to leave.'

She scoots across the tree house and takes my hand in hers.

'You have to understand I would never have been allowed to take Tom with me, Hannah. His father wouldn't have permitted it. That was never an option. So I did something terrible. I snatched at happiness for myself, but I left him with his father. And then I lied to Dad . . . or I never told him.'

'But why?' I brush my own tears away.

She squeezes my hand tighter. 'Because I was in love and still very young and, oh, Hannah, so stupid. I wanted him to think

I was perfect, not the kind of woman who would leave her child behind. And he would have insisted that he tried to help me to take Tom with us, to keep him, and that would never have happened. I'd have been made out to be an unfit mother, and your dad would have heard all of that in court and . . .' She shakes her head. 'I couldn't bear to be anything other than perfect for him. So I left Tom and I lied to your dad, and to all of you. I covered it up, even the divorce. I thought he'd be happy with his father — Tom was wanted very much and his father was so proud he had a son.'

'I don't get it, Mom. I can't imagine you ever leaving me or Jenny or Brandon. I don't understand.'

'This is very hard for me to say,' she replies, her hand knotted tight around mine. 'He wasn't like you and Jenny and Brandon, even as a little boy. There was always something unloving about him. I know what it's like to form a bond with your baby. With all of you, it was there from the beginning and I adored you more than I can ever put into words. And that's got stronger as you've all grown up, but it was just impossible with him. I did . . . love . . . him, but I never felt like I got anything back. He had the coldest way of looking at me sometimes.' She wipes her eyes again. 'I used to tell myself it was because of how I felt living in that house with his father.'

'Was it?'

Mom looks at me with your eyes, Jenny. Those big blue eyes

that helped tell Tom who you were. 'I don't know, sweetheart. And that's the truth. I just don't know.'

And there we are. Neither of us know why Tom was what he was. You might say it doesn't really matter, but we who are left behind need to know — it's like a compulsion without which we can't rest.

'I missed him,' Mom says quietly. 'Every day I thought about him and hoped he was OK. It's the price I paid for leaving. I was never really free.'

He's gone now, but we both know that she'll still never, ever be free.

In a way, Jenny, he has won.

CHAPTER 50

More than a year has passed, Jenny, since we brought you home. I've put flowers on your grave each week. I didn't want to end this until now because I was afraid of moving on. I don't want to leave you behind.

I'm up in the tree house. It's fall and the leaves are scattering across the grass below, carpeting it in reds and golds. We used to roll in them, do you remember? Cover ourselves with them and pretend to be fairy princesses in leaf dresses. Your hair would be spread out around you and you'd laugh and laugh as more leaves fell on top of you, blown by the breeze.

The air smells of fall too, with the promise of frosts and Hallowe'en hanging on it. I'm sheltered from the wind inside the tree house, snuggled up in a blanket, sipping coffee from a travel mug.

It has to be here that it ends, doesn't it? I know you'll understand that.

You would tell me to go on with life, Jenny. I'm more sure of that than I am of anything. And I will, but my memories of you are with me forever. There's some of you inside me that will never die. Nobody can take that away.

It's here too that I make another decision. I don't know if it's too late or if the thing I'm about to do is beyond stupid – if I'm investing in something that can never work. But Tom has destroyed enough lives. I've been thinking that, out of all the wreckage, something should be built.

I can almost hear you in here with me laughing and saying, 'About time.' Maybe I would have been quicker with you here to guide me, but I've had to grieve and heal, Jenny, and that takes a long time when you love someone as much as I love you.

You take a lot of getting over.

So I'm here to tell you that I choose life and I choose to fight. I don't think that will surprise you.

I fell in love with someone amazing and special. I fell in love with him because he's like the most perfect fit for me I can imagine. If there's a Hannah-shaped tessellating soul anywhere, then it is Harry's.

You would tell me not to let Tom win and you're right.

This is why I now take my phone and text Harry. It's been so long, at first, I don't know what to write.

And then I do. I'll reclaim those words and make something beautiful out of them. Something beautiful together. So I text him.

I need you. Please come.

ACKNOWLEDGEMENTS

My thanks for *In Another Life* go firstly to my editor at Egmont, Stella Paskins, for shaping the book from its raw form. As ever, her skill and insight makes all the difference. This is the only book I didn't write in a linear fashion and her sharp eyes were especially invaluable when I got too close to know where to make the cuts. To the rest of the team at Egmont, my additional thanks for all your hard work. To Jenny Hayes, who has now moved on, a big thanks for your care last summer when life got a touch frantic and difficult for a few months.

I owe my usual debt of gratitude to Ariella Feiner at United Agents for looking after me through another book, and for reminding me that juggling a full time career in education while looking after a baby and writing a book is quite a lot to do! Sometimes I forget that and only remember what I haven't done, rather than what I have. I tell anyone who ever asks me about agents that they are worth their weight in gold and then some, and Ariella is the reason why.

There is a special thank you to my husband, Paul, for *In Another Life*. We changed the plot of the book from the original idea and Paul was my sounding board for how to do this and came up with a rather good solution, which I think was much better than mine. He also found me my perfect location for Wolfscott.

And finally, my appreciation to all of my family for putting up with me during my usual writing process traumas of thinking I'm writing the worst book in the world ever and I'll never be able to finish it, etc. And they sweetly ignore me or nod and remind me that I've said exactly the same for every book I've ever written. Thanks for putting up with me – I love you all.

DON'T MISS . . .

Louder than Words

I can't speak the truth,
but I can write it

LAURA JARRATT

'This entire novel was astonishing, it's one
that won't ever leave me and touched me
more than any other book has. [It]
consumes you, mind, body and soul.'

SAFAH, GUARDIAN CHILDREN'S BOOKS

DON'T MISS . . .

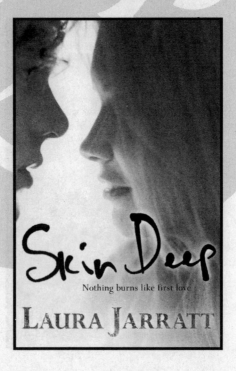

Skin Deep

Nothing burns like first love

LAURA JARRATT

Shortlisted for the Waterstones Book Prize and
Romantic Novelist's Association YA category

'Intensely romantic, really thrilling'
BOOKBAG

DON'T MISS . . .

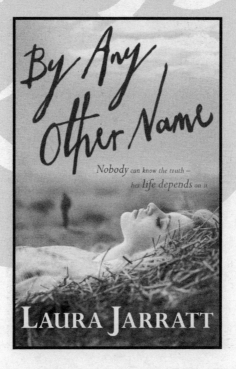

Nominated for the Carnegie Medal

'Edge of the seat stuff . . . absolutely terrific reading'

BOOKS MONTHLY